Gutted

Gutted

Justin Chin

Manic D Press
San Francisco

Cover photo © QiangBa DanZeng.

Some of these poems first appeared in different versions in *Shampoo*, *Mipo*, *Short Fuse: The Global Anthology of New Fusion Poetry* (Rattapallax Press).

Library of Congress Cataloging-in-Publication Data

Chin, Justin, 1969-
  Gutted / Justin Chin.
    p. cm.
Summary: "Within the Japanese poetic form of the *zuihitsu*, Chin reflects on
experiences of grief, loss, comfort and illness, and resolve"—Provided by publisher.
  ISBN-13: 978-1-933149-07-3 (pbk.)
  ISBN-10: 1-933149-07-8 (pbk.)
  I. Title.
PS3553.H48973G88 2006
811'.54—dc22
                          2006011857

Contents

In Memoriam

Dr. Chin Jeck Soon
18 June 1940 – 30 July 2003

Tonight, again

The sitting ghost is on attack again tonight.
He's twice as fitful, back again tonight.

When I wake from this, will I be a man or boy?
If this were *Flashdance*, we'd be hearing "Maniac" again tonight.

One hand plots murder, the other strains to understand.
The body's every sigh is sidetracked again tonight.

Call out the National Guard; evacuate the trolls to safe ground.
I'm matchbook & gasoline, I'm burning bridges in stacks again tonight.

Greyhound, rabbit, pony, racehorse, NASCAR, motocross.
Hope take one more fluttering spin on the racetrack again tonight.

Those limp wrists beget such limp applause.
There'll be no encore for the egomaniac again tonight.

I gave the conductor my fare, I've got my transfer.
I'm ready to climb on board the wagon again tonight.

I'm slipping down the barrel of this pigpen.
Looks like it's bareback again tonight.

The things that give you pleasure are someday going to hurt you.
Are you ready to flail & fail and take some flak again tonight?

Under all the sand in the Sahara, all the fossils melting into oil.
How can these bones lay down their arms afield again tonight?

All these flags, rotting red white & blue on cars, walls & poles.
These are personal wounds, flown to staunch the ache again tonight.

Under all the clodded dirt of mass graves & cemeteries,
When can these bones rest in arms unweary & appeased again tonight?

In the peaceable kingdom, the lion & the lamb may lie together.
But on earth, their each own lies aren't worth a quack again tonight.

In grieving, how frightfully far is the sea to shining sea.
Every day's every incomplete mourning affects again tonight.

We pray so that God knows He exists.
Who should be blamed for His lack again tonight?

Dexammethazone, cyclopamine, vincristine, rebetol, interferon, temodar.
Acyclovir, stemastil, neutrophil, tamoxifan, teslac again tonight.

What's next, what's next, and then, and then.
Blah blah blah, over and over, again and again, again tonight.

A liturgy of how we fell; a list of obstacles that trip.
O Litterbugs! Is all this payback a gain tonight?

I'm never quite as good as when I bleed.
I won't deny the hypochondriac again tonight.

Burgundy for sex, Bordeaux for intellect.
The wino looks for a corkscrew in the haystack again tonight.

The heart's blackmarket trades in things unknown to us.
Here's my left-ass, may I have another whack again tonight?

Crucify or complain, but the needle's found the vein.
Tell me, while we're waiting, all the drawbacks again tonight.

The exile describes, remembers, then imagines.
His dreaming interrupted by flashbacks again tonight.

We invest all our cracked eggs into one omelet.
How much interest did Mr. Banker gain tonight?

Riding the mule to look for the White Horse.
Guess who's the insomniac again tonight?

I pulled the cord, signaled the driver to slow down, to stop.
I want to get off the wagon, find my tracks again tonight.

What are the limits of one's grief, of what one creature can bear?
Who will witness how it eats your heart as a snack again tonight?

When the road map doesn't continue on E16, Pg. 45 nothing.
Strong lifelines on such tiny hands: I predict a wreck again tonight.

My spectacular failures, my holy spooks, my brilliant bugaboos.
Hold on, little boy, you're going to bruise like heck again tonight.

Book One

THE FATHER, THE SON

Gutted

My favorite children's bedtime prayer
is the one that goes:

> Matthew, Mark, Luke and John,
> The bed be blest that I lie upon,
> Four angels to my bed,
> Four angels around my head,
> One to watch and one to pray,
> And two to bear my soul away.

This is such a vast improvement
over the more popular,

> Now I lay me down to sleep,
> I pray the Lord my soul to keep.
> If I should die before I wake,
> I pray the Lord my soul to take.

The difference is that
in one, you get to go
to bed with four men.

But in both, the child is afraid
he will die in the middle
of the night in his sleep.

> (Why? What's going on in these homes?
> Where's Child Protective Services when they're needed?)

Later, the child will grow up
and realize the lie hidden
in those prefabricated prayers.

That is what most people want:
to die in your sleep,
to die in your own bed.

Given the choice between a cold well-lit room
or a warm dark one, the red-tipped long-winged beetles
swarm to the light bulb tundra
and crippling death.

Would we humans choose any different?

How we clearly see. How we secret safe.
What difference does it become

in the dusty vacuum belly
of the Black & Decker Dustbuster?

(directions)

I've told you
once before
not to ask
Gertrude Stein
for directions.
We need
to get
there
by suppertime.

One day at home, I came through the door
and found my grandmother sitting on the sofa
in front of the television crying.
"What happened?" I asked. I was concerned.

She had, all afternoon, been watching
a Discovery channel documentary:
the migration of the wildebeests.

The wildebeesties in their annual migration
had to splash their way across a crocodile infested river,
many were savagely snacked on by the crocs
who lurked waiting, disguised as floating debris with peepers.

This upset her gravely.
"Why doesn't the government build a bridge for them?" she asks me.

At my grandmother's wake, my father was asked
to say a few words. He was a surprise.
My dad, he, the archetypical stoic Chinese father,
in so few mumbly words, in such a simple direct way,
was all at once genuine and heartfelt, funny and sorrowful.

He had insisted on wearing his tan golf shorts
to the funeral, until my mother intervened and
a pair of dark gray trousers was dug out of my suitcase,
hemmed with safety pins and duct tape.

He was saved from being the most inappropriately dressed
by my cousin who works for MTV Asia, and who showed up
in a midriff-baring outfit. Her mother later apologizes for her.
"Her clothes all don't have the middle part," she tells us.

Lawn as far as the eye can see
under this honey lake of sky.

Day's unlooming light drapes
the manicured green of the 18th hole.

There is a short athletic man surveying the putt.
There is a woman with him. Or a drag queen.

The man is my father.
And this is Heaven.

The woman, I'm not quite sure of.
I lean in to take a closer look.

"Dad! Does Mom know you're playing golf with Celia Cruz?"

There is a fairway in Heaven simply
because this is my father's Heaven.

Celia Cruz is here because she died
the same day and of the same illness.

I'm here because I want to believe
that I would be a part of his heaven.

I want my father's heaven to be wholly his,
brimful with all the joy and pleasure denied him

in the last 18 months of his life.
But I cannot reckon the dribble for the waterfall.

I cannot see the gnashing flood
in the cup of water I hold in hand.

Before he was my father,
he was his own Bible and roadmap.

Did he see all he wanted
to see in his life?

How much of himself did he relinquish
at the painted foot of my crib?

Deprived of light by the drama of my shadow puppets,
how many of his dreams withered to naught beneath?

Who would he have been unyoked,
unburdened, and then some?

I pray I should never know, nor
do I dare feign to imagine.

In my father's heaven, there is always
three-in-one coffee served in old-time kopi-tiam cups.

There is good unfussy food; his friends
and brothers and sisters are coming for dinner.

There is no complicated civil service to navigate
nor corrupt bureaucracy to fandangle with.

The woman he loved so faithfully for 38 years,
whose face he knew he would wake to every morning

would be there, of course, in due time.
There is opera and music; common sense abounds.

His tee-off time is confirmed in the book;
he has a good bed with an extra soft pillow

to put over his head when he sleeps,
just the way he likes it. He dreams well;

I do not seek to disturb his forty
winking. I pray, I hope:

in the dizzying carnival of his dreamland,
there will be one single blade of grass

with my name, what he
long ago chose for the baby

in his hands,
written on it.

Even if life has left – captivity, crowding (surely, despair) will do that – it should still be heavy for its size. Slide your finger in, under, and test the flesh for bounce, elasticity; check for cracks and discoloration, these are to be avoided; shine, desirable.

But life is preferable to lifeless. Select the feisty. Those with some fight. Wrap them in wet newspapers, you want their blood to stay warm, even in the fridge. Never, but if you must, ice then vacuum seal in freezer bags while still green.

But in all states, it should smell like sweet brine, like the sea from whence it was plucked. Ask a fisherman, a doctor, a housewife, a refugee, a day laborer, a relief worker, a navyman, a pirate, what the sea smells like.

This was the year my best friend Lisa and I
were completely obsessed with O magazine,
we especially enjoyed the puzzles in them.
Okay, they were really self-esteem improvement
self-actualization quizzes and worksheets,
             but they were so puzzling.
There is a regular section "What I Know For Sure"
and that one had me stumped for weeks
before I moved on to other obsessions.
I just could not make a list of things
that I *really* knew for sure, and then
I wasn't even sure if I knew that for sure.

I was looking at other people's personal web-pages.
I was fascinated by their Frequently Asked Questions page.
It made me realize how different,

                         how set apart I have become.
The questions I am frequently asked are:
         "Omigawd! *What* have you done?"
         "Who are you and what are you doing in my room?"
         "Why are you so selfish and wicked and hateful?"
         "How long do you think you can cling to your tissue of lies?"
         "Are you sure that isn't infected?"
         "Why can't you just accept the inevitable?"

Recently, whilst cleaning out my desk drawers, I found
a copy of an online questionnaire I had filled out.
One of the questions asked:
             If you could pick one super-human power
             (such as comic-book characters have)
             what would you choose?[1]

---

1. If you recognize the question, it *is* from match.com. Small mitigation, but I was there merely stalking someone, hence making it just ever so slightly less pathetic than being there to actually find a hook-up.

I had answered:
The luxury of having someone else
write the script to a two-dimensional recyclable life,
the ability to cope with the daily accumulation
of pain & grief & helplessness & despair;
     –or–
super-blasting death-rays (either in honeydew or cherry-red,
but it would be most cool if there was some way
you could adjust and customize the colors,
say, with a slider in the preferences panel)
that shoot out of my nostrils.

Yes, people expect it to come out of the eyes,
so they'll never expect the nostrils.
    Unfortunately, I will be useless
or at the very least horribly messy during allergy season.

My slow years
folded up

like pairs
of jeans

on the shelf
at The Gap

piled one
on another

a totem

      the floundering size-36 years
      the naïve fearless size-28 years

all folded
to the same
proportions

      on display
      in storage.

(services)

So I hear
you do weddings

                    now,
what a coincidence

          I do baptisms.

We should
find someone

who does exorcisms,

            open a small office
            at the new strip mall.

How many roads must a man walk down,
before he can scratch the rosea of his gray itch?

This itchy malaise logged
by phantom limbs' frequent flier miles

straddling all those dreams:
abandoned, curbed, crushed; unattainable.

"In times of crisis, we must all decide again and again whom we love."
— Frank O'Hara, *To the Film Industry in Crisis*

Lately I've been thinking
about the longstanding nature
of love and of happiness and all that stuff.
About my life as it stands
held together with little bits of string.

In my early life, my need to belong
and my need for security made me accept
such stupid and lethal conditions.
    In my later life, I should have known
better but the stupid and lethal stuff
was always the most fun.

When I was of that age, I thought
the question coming was to be:
        "What have I done with my life?"
        "How will I be remembered?"

Now, that I am at the age, I realize
the question should have been, and was always:
        "What have I done to my life?"
        "How will I be forgotten?"

A thousand and one
monkeys pounding
away at one thousand
and one iMacs.

Oh no,
this morning
one monkey
called in sick.

Twelve

It takes Jupiter 12 years to make a full orbit of the Sun.

The life expectancy of a game cat in captivity is 12 years. Its life expectancy in the wild will depend on its wiliness, drought and brush fires, the luxuriousness of its coat, the aphrodisiac qualities of its paw or penis, and whether it is the theme ingredient on *Iron Chef*.

A coconut palm takes 12 years to bear fruit. When the fruit ripens, you pluck and cut into it, and taste, you will find that you've spent twelve years waiting for rats to pee in your mouth.

The feud between the Hatfields and the McCoys lasted 12 years. The television series based on it lasted 5 years; the biennial convention that worships each major and minor creak and crevice of that series continues till today.

It is said that Leonardo DaVinci spent 12 years painting the Mona Lisa's lips. At the Louvre, the snaking line to see those lips will run you 12 minutes during peak hours, less than three during off-peak. In front of the portrait, you will hear in any variety of languages, "Is that it?"

A wingless bug in Fremont, California, power-walking at a centimeter per minute, would take 12 years to get to San Francisco's Union Square, assuming it doesn't get squished on the Bay Bridge. If the bug crawls onto public transit, and it will need a transfer, the journey time is shortened considerably.

Twelve dog years roughly equals 61 human years; twelve cat years, though, are 64. Who has the more stressful life?

What do you want to forget in 12 years? Start now.

Put your hand on your heart. There is a small rest between each heartbeat. In the course of an ordinary lifetime, the human heart — even with palpitations, no matter how many horror movies you see, cheap shocks foisted upon you, no matter how many zero-gravity rollercoaster g-force-plunging thrill rides, marathons and triathlons, mountains climbed, no matter how much methamphetamine, step-aerobics, heartbreak or heart-attack you take on – stands still for, give or take a little, 12 years.

Put your hand on your heart. Every thump you feel is counting down, one more down, to its last beat, that last squeeze.

(How We Might Perish)

Tripping over landmines,
decapitation by clothesline, resurgence
of swine flu, snapped
spine, war wounds, whacked
by goons, floods during
monsoon, homicidal maniac, bulimia
by ipecac, mainlining tainted
smack, cardiac attack, gored
by yak in heat,
cat poop parasites, stroke,
spider bite (brown recluse),
white phosphorous sweep, in
your sleep, ill-timed base-jump
leap, fanatical believer wielding
meat cleaver, advanced Dengue
Fever, hangman's noose, acute
polysubstance abuse, E-coli tainted
juice, U.N. sanctions, SARS,
staph superinfection, malaria, electrocution,
malnutrition, falling litter, cirrhosis
of liver, cancer (assorted),
killer bees, plane crash,
septicemia, brain aneurysm, mutating
strain of flu, SUV
rollover, hypertension, crushed in
earthquake, stress, anxiety attack.

My grandfathers did not live long enough
to see their grandchildren grow up.
One never knew I was to exist and the other,
who really was my great-grandfather,
had me thrust upon him at the nursing home,
long enough for two photos to be taken.
His mental state so deteriorated
he could have been holding a sack of drooling yams
for all that it mattered.
And it did to those taking the photograph.
The other felled by a stroke at his butchershop,
came back grumpy, iron-fisted and older-fashioned.
He doted on us, his grandsons;
we were teens, half-formed blobs,
and he never saw who we would become, or how we would.

My father did not live long enough to see his
only grandchild grow up.
            (He would not even know of the others
             down the line, nor they of him.)

And at some pin-prick point in time,
this little sweetness of a child
will have no real memory of her grandfather
or later, of me.

She will wonder who her grandfather was,
not remembering how he beamed Cheshire Cat-like
whenever she was around, how he carried and doted on her
like he never did with his own children,
how he lugged her kiddie table across two statelines
strapped to the roof of his car, how he drove
105 miles to get her favorite shoes specially re-soled.

She will wonder who this uncle of hers was,
not remembering that soap bubble-blowing toy monkey

from Camden Market that caused two full-scale baggage searches
at two airports, and how delighted she was
lying in front of Bubble Monkey while he did his thing.
Will she remember the swimming lessons? the games of shark-horsey?
or the bedtime stories he made up,
and how for weeks she kept searching for those stories
in all her books, insisting to her father
that the stories were there. Will she remember
the tireless hours he spent playing tea party with her?
Or will she outgrow those tea parties and ballet-dancing mice,
forsake them in favor of the mall and best friends,
lipsticks and nylons;
                        and I'll be dimmed,
worn as a Post-it note, the writing in an unfamiliar hand,
on its last sticks, barely clinging
to a basket of already broken,
dis-used and outgrown toys.

Two Answers,
four questions, one statement of fact, three useless
useless platitudes, and one unfinished thought,
          to be exact. Which,
of course, you should punctuate accordingly before use:

I can travel anywhere with additional pain

I was willing to be easy but then things got complicated so damn
quickly

The slow sad waltz of my favorite perversion

The theory goes that there are only four kinds of suffering and two
kinds of joy that exists in the entire world
We just pass them around back and forth, on eBay, at flea markets, and in
the dust we inhale

What is anthropology but apology with its or nth degree
What is shellfish but selfish

If it's not butter, it can be fried in butter

How mesmerizing is that montage of cats falling off television sets, backs
    of sofas, kitchen tables, and assorted shelving units

Does invincibility have more to do with persistence rather than the
possession of superhuman traits or is it dumb luck

Like telling an ant it is a lion, but an antlion is something else altogether

Like eating a really good hamburger on the sluicing floor of the abattoir

Shit in a bag and punch it
Walk a mile in my clogs on your hands and knees

For the version of how things will end we have yet to write
Who's to say how this won't end

Oh look,
a typo

in the
Rosetta Stone.

"The black cells will dry up and die
Or sing with joy and have their way.
They breed so quietly night and day,
You never know, they never say."
— Harold Pinter, *Cancer Cells*

When she said *Edema*,
I immediately thought

in my head   *Edamame.*

>   Little green soybean
>   taking swollen root
>   in an estrogen lattice
>   swell.

Edema takes its root
from *Oedipal*, which I'm told,
in the 16th Century, meant,
            'really great at solving difficult
            riddles, puzzles and word jumbles'

not 'creepy motherfucker.'

For months, we had been trying to get Dad to agree to move cross country to my brother's home where there could be more support services and family to help, and for Mom's waning sanity, even if she did not see herself turning into fungus. For months, he shrugged off the suggestion.

Then one day, he said, "Okay, let's go." Just like that.

I packed them up. My brother drove the 250 miles to pick them up.

The first day in my brother's house, my dad received his old high school friends who had chartered a bus so they could travel to visit him all together. Oh, how they talked and reminisced and laughed. The floors shook and the walls trembled with life. The second day, he spent playing with his granddaughter. And on the third day, he fell in and out of consciousness and then, he died.

A month before my grandmother died, we had asked what her plans were for that year's church camp. She said, "Maybe I don't want to go this year, maybe I want to go somewhere better." We thought she meant Perth, Australia. After all, "somewhere better" than the Prinsep Street Presbyterian Annual Church Camp summoned up a rather lengthy list of destinations and activities.

A week before she died, in a moment of confusion, she went around the house looking for me. When she could not find me, she called my mom, who told her I was still in the U.S. and was not scheduled to come home till the end of the year. My grandmother then proceeded to wash a pair of shoes I left behind on the shoe-rack, scrubbing and blancoing them the way she used to wash my school shoes during primary school; and later, when someone was home to help her dial, she calls to tell me she's washed my shoes. It was a pair of white hi-tops that I had not worn in more than eight years. I tell her so, "White Hi-Tops! What...? Do I live in Belgium?" We have a good long chat. The night before she died, she wondered again where I was.

They said that people who are about to die, somehow know it. Nurses and health care professionals have all testified to it, too.

What must that knowing feel like? What must that feel like in your gut? Is it a sudden realization or something that gradually reveals itself? How are you sure it's not just acid reflux? Or gas?

The specialist tells me that my dad is not in any pain.
The medications will take care of that.

But what does that final act actually feel like?

Twice, I seriously thought I was going to die. In each case, copious amounts of narcotics were involved and in each case, I was never so much in pain as much as an aching sadness, just a melancholy that drew a line to my brain: I knew I had done something really wrong and really bad. I wasn't frightened. All I felt was foolish and sad.

The four times I have been dragged to the E.R. in blinding pain — each its own special agony — each time, I was nowhere even close to death, even as it felt like I was; and the rupturing appendix on the fourth trip was about to cross that line. The reward for staying so far away from that light is even more hours of scorching pain while the doctors and nurses try to figure it out, inject dye into you, force radiated chalky fluids down your throat, send you around the ward in 80 days for scans and ultrasounds and blood work.

During the year of blinding fatigue, I once fell into a deep afternoon nap where I was taken by night terrors, except this was late afternoon. Sitting ghosts, we called them, malevolent forces who hold you down, frozen and unable to move or sit on your chest so that you could not breathe, for what reasons we never know. This time, I decided to rage against the fearful force and so I did. Pushing and fighting, and just as suddenly, I was adrift, in the air soaring like a songbird let out of its cage, gliding up towards the sky and into a dazzling white light. "It's not a good idea to fly into the light," I suddenly realized, and in the instant of realization, I awoke. The TV was on, Mary Hart on *Entertainment Tonight* was announcing that Tom Cruise and Nicole Kidman had just split up.

(portamento)

Her piano teacher, she said, told her to keep playing
even if mistakes were made.

                              Mine however, kept
a half-foot wooden dressmaker's ruler hovering
above the hands on the keys, ready to strike
misfingerings,
            miscues, wrong notes,
                        unmusic. Fingers
                              being as fingers are,
mistakes were make.

We learned *portamento*;

just as our violin cousins in adjoining studios
learned *vibrato*;
                        under the crushing threat
imposed by needlenose pliers.

                  The music continued.

This is a picture of barely feathered baby birds chirping. The motherbird is standing on the overhanging branch trilling in musical singsong.

You're reading into it, imposing your will. It is a picture. There is no sound nor soundtrack. How can you actually be sure the birds are chirping?

Their beaks are open.

The birds may be gasping for air. Pollution is such a problem in these gas-guzzler days.

There are musical notes issuing from their beaks. Look, see, here is the wavy staff, see, here are semi-quavers, a dangling sharp.

If you played those notes on a recorder or a piano, on an accordion or even a church organ, you will hear a piteous sound. Discordant ugly stuff, vile, nauseous; nothing as chirping is chirpy.

Even an ugly tune is still music. And chirpy is as chirp is.

Have it your way then. This will be your chirp.

I chirp.

The makeshift raft barely holding
together barely afloat carrying
forty destitute refugees
fleeing civil unrest and famine
comes wave crest to shoreline
with the opulent clothing optional
exclusive resort.

Misery meets Luxury.

The naked and tanned
are bringing food and fruit
and Evian to the beach.

(…life completed…)

The world's suffering
lay by your lovely
feet clad
in high-tech sneakers.

Take your shoes off if you dance on furniture.
Wear them if you want to walk on a bed of roses.

See the flower farm in year-long harvest:
How such delicate blossoms
cause such misery, so much hardship?

(...life interrupted...)

Incontinence

Looking back on that late morning, when it was just
the two of us in the house, perhaps watching
that meandering and indulgent documentary
on waterslide parks in the Middle East,
                oil creating such magnificently
                excessive unnatural bodies of water
                in the middle of a blistering desert,
was clearly not the best idea.

Even as we sat there, even before
I heard the faint drip to the floor,
the runoff trickled around the crevices,
the cracks of the sofa, I knew
something was afoot.

I knew what the medications did to the bladder.
I also knew shame, and embarrassment,
and face.

                "natural given the treatment"
                "no problem cleaning it up"
                "nothing to be ashamed of"
                "never mind, it's okay"

Self-consciousness cloaks itself
with clichés, a fashion victim,
wearing layers upon layers thick
of ill-matched garments,
inappropriate for the present weather.

I know.
There are days, low days
when the meds abrade against my appetites,
and accidents will happen, in spite
of best efforts.

And any dignity that you can hand back
to someone who has just crapped his pants in public
is not a dignity of a kind that anyone can use,
or should want. You're getting the placebo
in a medical trial for tainted medicine.

I know
to keep watching
the mile-long waterslide that even
lets you slide upwards by virtue of powerful jets
strategically placed.

Now, he's in the bathroom, quietly changing into fresh clothes.

Now, he's in the back kitchen
trying to put the soiled clothes
into the washing machine or a wash pail of water,
but the machine is running, there are no available pails.

Now, he's found the air freshener under the sink; later
he will go to his room to nap, and I will leg in
on my hands and knees and clean up so that not
a smudge will be known when the others get home.

Now, he's back in the bathroom,
bundling his soiled clothes in a sheaf
of old newspapers and cramming that
into a plastic grocery bag.

And I just again want to be the one
who fell asleep in the stands with his head
in his dad's lap at the home team's first game
on home ground to a capacity crowd;

            close my eyes and lay my head down
            in the swell of boisterous noise and all
            hullabaloo, open them
            in the still quiet of my room,
            tucked into bed.

(Petit Mal)

A little evil, a small illness.
Why does it sound like pastry?

And vaguely remember incorrectly,
a euphemism for orgasm,
which is neither evil nor ill.

Is any evil so little, illness so small
that it ceases to be wicked and ill?

Oh, now I see what it does to a body.

Yes, it is evil. Small is relative.
Illness all.

I always thought that my death
would somehow involve wildebeests.
But I now know that is unlikely to happen
unless I take matters into my own hands.

Why wait for the shit to hit the fan?
Take some initiative, pick the shit up
and fling it at the fan yourself.
I find that an overhand throw
is best for doing this.

I would say that I throw like a girl,
but that is meaningless and wholly sexist.
No, I throw like a gay man
whose muscles have atrophied from an unrelenting year
of chemotherapy and fatigue.

There are people who are sick.
There are people who are ill.
There is a difference.

These have been long and difficult years
and nothing in my life has prepared me
for how to cope. But a body copes
and man, how it does.
                                    I can tolerate
another year of this fatigue. I can take those
25-hour flights there and 25-hour flights back
without 40 much less 12 winks.
I can plan a funeral for forty.

What will kill me
will be the small things:
I cannot bear to wash another plate,
to sweep the floor, to change the sheets.
            But I have to because I fell asleep

while having dinner in bed watching telly.
Mid-chew burrito I passed out
and when I woke, early morning hours later
all the lights on, the cat sprawled
all over the mess of beans & rice & blankets.

    While cleaning up,

    I wept.

I will not rouse the sleeping or the dead.
Who falls further, the weeping or the dead?

It's not how far you fall, but how you land.
Are you here for the sowing, reaping, or the dead?

Why ask for an arm, a leg but not a butt
        to fall back on? These road urges
will want to sleep in floods.

When rust crushes into iron,
like water chained to honey,
a thousand aches

            manipulate this elaborate symphony.

*"When they come to the Grave, while the Corpse is made ready to be laid into
the earth, shall be sung or said:* In the midst of life we are in death: of
whom may we seek for succour, but of thee, O LORD, who for our sins
art justly displeased?" — *1789 U.S. Book of Common Prayer*

(vincristine)

The first time I met Vincristine
she was sally in the veins, flowing
in blood like persuasion.

What I now remember:
Clothed in a clot of near-neon, the color
was Green Cream Soda, brought to market
by Frasier & Nieve to limited success.

We drank it because we loved
the icky color, the Vesuvian foam
that unfailingly shot
up the bottle neck
          made a mess
whenever the cap was popped.

The taste
we put up with
too sweet, stinging
          indescribable
though we sensed some faraway
familiar   periwinkle
                             the beginning of nausea
                nothing
we ever wanted

to seek
on our own.

I would not mind getting the cancer
that Ali MacGraw gets in *Love Story*,
the cancer where as you lay dying,
you become more beautiful and more moisturized.

The classic death would be Garbo's *Camille*,
but all that coughing and flopping around on the bed
is just so undignified. I realize she had consumption,
but at least Nicole Kidman in *Moulin Rouge*
still managed to karaoke with her consumption.

I certainly wouldn't want the cancer
Debra Winger gets in *Terms of Endearment*.
"Come to Laugh, Come to Cry, Come to Care, Come to Terms."
Oh, just go away already.

The death I would most like
is Bette Midler's in *The Rose*.
Where, up on stage in front of a packed house,
I'll tell the story of the first time I heard
the blues, and as the story winds down,
my speech all slurry and raised to an odd minor chord,
I'll wonder, Why is it so dark? Who turned off all the lights? Where has
everybody gone?
                              Then I will collapse and die.[1]

My one request for my funeral
is that at no point should "I Believe I Can Fly"
be sung, played, hummed, mumbled, muttered,
mentioned or thought of.
                 This is how poltergeist activity gets started.

But I know, I know my death
                 will not kill me.
Rather it is the death of others
                 that will kill me.

---

1. While the strains of "The Rose" play in the background. I want the version that is a
duet with Bette Midler and Wynonna Judd. That is the gayest rendition ever. Before
you even get to the second verse, before you find out that the one who won't be taken
cannot seem to give or that love is only for the lucky and the strong, you just want to
be fucked up the arse.

(good grief)

Why is it so dark?
Who turned off all the lights?
Where has everybody gone?

When did the meter become the meter, or a yard
a yard, or even an inch an inch,
so that I could take a mile, or for that matter
a centimeter or two.

> "At the bottom of every frozen heart, there is a drop or two of love, just
> enough to feed the birds." — Henry Miller, *Tropic of Cancer*

Don't go to the doctor.

Grief is accurate. Grief is not accurate.
Do you want to know the facts or do you want
the details?

Here's what you will need. Listen carefully.

Something for when you need help seeing the things close
at hand and the things far at hand.

Something to measure whether the mess was worth the sickly
pile or even that very last mile.

Why name something when you can just point at it.
Use a laser pointer or a twig if your finger refuses

to work with your brain. Some things
should take care of themselves,

they should need you and not
need you.

Not only remember, but remember
to help yourself forget

    [and here I cannot read my handwriting, it is so scrawled,
      so small, but soon expands, broadening

    in its whoops and mad codes,
      its abbreviated hiccoughing,

    its hacking inadequate cursive.]

Hashima

This deliciously chilled
sweet gelatinous dessert.

We could not agree
nor ascertain whether

it was:
frog semen?
        a colony of frogs
        sitting on individual lilypads
        wanking away

or was it
frog sputum?
        an army of frogs
        their long sticky tongues
        wrapped around webbed digits
        puking up
        into half walnut shells
        their own little spittoons.

No one else was quite so sure either:
    Reconstituted frog saliva
    Snow Frog Glands   which secretes copious amounts
    Frog brains   of fat which is sorely needed
    Pregnant frog placenta   for hibernating
    Frog fallopian tubes
    Toad womb   Frog it turned out to be.
    Snow Frog blubber   *Rana chensinensis.*
    Frog stomach   And only from
    Toad fat   the Jelin Changbai Mountains.
    Frog eggs

    What we ate. *Ranae Oviductus.*
    The fat surrounding the oviducts.

Touted as having 16 of the 18 essential amino acids,
five of which are said not found in any other food,

"moistens the lungs"   and as a cure for any ache or ill

                              post-partum lethargy, t.b. & asthma,
                              kidney disease, cancer
                              immune system disorders.

Second only to bird's nest.   The spit of swallows that collect in their
                               twiggy nest.

For those who can't afford
or can't stomach   Local entrepreneurs have been
bird spit.   gutting a room in the second or third
                               level of their homes, making little
                               crevices & nooks hoping it would prove
                               tempting to the swallows to nest there,
                               drool there.

The notion unsurprisingly
brings up the oogies in the West.
          Oh those people! They'll eat anything
          that has its back to the sun!
Swallow spit, mountain frog ovary fat.
                              Is honey any different?

How far stung is the rash of hope that makes
medicine out of the vile? How much sweet
                    is worth sacrificing
for the remotest possibility
                    of wholeness, the impulse to nourish
weighed against the vile?
Ick for ick, who quantifies the foul?
                    what sort of calipers are used?

Does it go down better, imported
                    and rechristened: Snow Jelly.

(snow)

Coming from warmer climes
the peppering snowfall outside the window
still evoked romance and sentimental daydreams
even as the temperature dropped and frostbite threatened.
Come December, and the whitest Christmas
will be found in shopping malls across Southeast Asia,
countries lying in a perspiring clutch
on the equator. With no real experience of snow
but for the undefrosted freezer, the imagination
soars to Antarctic heights.

What did we learn in English 101, Poetry subsection?
                              Snow: blankets and covers everything.
                              a classic trope for death/renewal,
                              also Fall/Autumn
                              Romance.
            (we dutifully wrote in the Norton margins
            in pencil so as to not mar the sellback value)

Fluffy snowfall or blizzard.
Romantic, and then turns dangerous.

It also preserves,
one of the properties of it icy nature,

but preservation only comes after
the kill.

The Keeper of Memories

There was still the keeper of memories to contend with.

It's how the middle class remembers, someone once told him.

Memory as a coefficient of disappointment, he said.

These were what he was permitted to forget:

No one asking the homewrecker what sort of home it was to begin with.

The ex-girlfriend's haircut at the United baggage carousel.

No more like a willow shall he bend.

Kidnapped by the Yeti.

These were what he was permitted to remember:

Fishbone stuck in throat.

How a sentence changes in time, with time, and becomes something altogether different.

Eye-glazing naval-gazing wool-gathering.

The disintegrating time.

These, he was still unsure of; their status was still being seriously considered:

How one corpse cares for another in the decline.

The seven deadly scenes.

These, he knew, he could never forget:

The dream in which God is vengeful.

The dream in which God is forgiving.

All summer it springs forth.

Suicidal ideation.

How should one not fall.

Medicine to cure will do this.

Irony? or HMO?

It's getting too dark for me to see.

(Leaving Sodom and Gomorrah)

I've got
the Triple Sec
& the Cuervo Gold.
When we get
to that lime grove,
can you look
back and see
how many guests
we might expect?

One, the generously affectionate stray who stayed.

Two, the thug with the split ear and alley ways who tormented the first one.

Three, the black and gray tabby with the crook in his tail that straightened in his old age.

Four, the one now, the handsome one with the tail curl not unlike Kim Novak's hairbun in *Vertigo*, who will talk to you, have whole conversations even; for him the bed is the safest place he knows; "something about saving each other".

And five, my white-socked mild-mannered friend, bookends to a third of my life, where I was gung-ho and callow I grew into my doubt and damage; who faithfully sat on the pillow by my head all those weeks when I could not get out of bed; she placed her purr in the palm of my hand. Those years, that summer, my heart knew its duty, it was swathed in gray fur.

The Last

This is the last time I will be in the house I grew up in. This is
the last time I will hear your voice. This is the last family
portrait where everyone is present. This is the last Christmas,
the last Christmas present, the last tub of Brylcreem
you will get in your stocking. This is the last family dinner, the last
acid reflux I will ever stomach. This is the last time anything

will taste this good. This is the last calibration
of my tongue; after this, every spoonful of food, every sip of drink,
every sliver of a kiss will taste like gun-metal. This is
the last scoop of chocolate chip ice cream I will scoop for you.
This is the last time you will see my impression of the Anopheles mosquito
landing on skin, notice the bend in the leg, notice the precision

in my stance. This is the last time you will be offended by my dirty feet,
the last time you will complain that I do not wash them properly. This is
the last bout of gout. The last dental appointment. The last pill I will need
to take. This is the last piece of the jigsaw puzzle, and now the picture
is complete: night sky, matte black, we thought,
but there are two stars, or might they be planets, on that last piece.

This is the last time I will see my father alive. The last time you might see
me alive. This is the last thing you saw before you fell
asleep last night, but it was not the first thing you saw when you awoke
this morning. This is the last sunset in Paris you will see, and the last
time I will be amazed at how a sky can be so violet
for so long. This is your last ever coo of awe. This

is the last full day of carefree you will know. The last time I make
the same careless mistake again. This is the last
list I will ever make. The last one I would not adhere to.
This is the last scrap from the table. Oh, what a gluttonous feast
we've missed. This is the last note in the soundtrack of your life.
There is no replay button, no encore; you will, however, learn

to live with the silence. This is the last piece to the puzzle you've long
given up trying to solve. This is your last will and testament.

This is the last celebrity chimpanzee you will have to endure.
This is the last impression you will leave on me. And oh! what
a lasting one it will be. This is the last orbit of all
your imaginary satellites. You are no longer the sun, you have no

gravitational pull anymore. This is the last dance, let's dance this
last dance for love. This is the last exit, the final exit; I am going
to miss the off ramp if you keep distracting me. This is the last software
upgrade, the last illegal download, the last sidetrack you will need.
This is the last time a song you hear on the radio will exactly
encapsulate your feelings, or will seem dirty or sexy. This is the last

non-sequitor to make sense, the last time nonsense will ever contain
an unthawed jewel of sense. This is the last hunger
pang, the last roil of jealously, the last feeling of inadequacy. This is
the last time you will be first. The last time you will be
the first to know, the first to believe, the first to fall.
This is the last temptation. There will be no more trials after this one.

This is the last jellyfish sting anyone will ever
suffer; they are all extinct now, they were delicious.
This is the last time sequential order makes sense; the last
time you use π, the last calculation. This is the last time you will look
like yourself, healthy, normal, like how you want people
to remember you, before the steroids puffed you up, before the meds

gave you a hump, wasted your heft away. This is the last time
I can truly say I am clean. This is the last of our demons.
From now on, you will fear nothing that cannot be seen or named.
From now on, I will fear everything that you do not fear.
This is the last stretch, the last free ride, the last open
road, I will be taking public transit, and you,

you will probably hitchhike from here on. Even as we both have nowhere
to go, no place to be. This is the last time you can tell anyone this
is the house you moved into a week before your 7th birthday.
This is the last time you can sit beside the mango tree in the backyard
over where the first cat you ever called your own was buried. It is not your
garden anymore and this is the last time you will ever have a backyard

or a garden. This is the last time anything lasted this long and felt
this good and made such sense and you thought it would never end,
or that it would surely return someday soon. This is where you get
the last laugh; take it graciously. This is the last vestige
of your youthful invincibility, your vain glorious
visions of your future, your fearless swagger. This is the last

sashay of my fearless swagger. My sagging ass will never
announce its arrogance with such perkiness again.
                                        And at last,
what really lasts? The material buckles and collapses, lifetimes
teeter and implode. The inertia thickens and every little speck
gyres to this last measure, this endgame of cul-de-sacs
and open-all-night black-holes; this end; where

everything ends. The cowboy frees his horse into the lush
green meadow, lays his pistols down, and strolls off
into the sunset. But walks smack face-first
into the ultra-realistic backdrop of a movie lot.
Red-faced, he tries to walk back onto what
he now realizes is a set, a set-up. He tries to reclaim

his role as hero, but his trusty steed is long gone, his pistols
rusted beyond salvage. All he has is a charley horse and bullets
that don't fit in any gun's barrel. He has boxes and crates
of those. And now, the set is in decay, paint peeling
and chipped, dusty and tarnished, falling down in heaves; the builders
have emigrated to shinier worlds, the costumers and wardrobe ladies are on

strike; all they have left behind is a barnful of tumbleweed.
So apropos for this rapidly incipient ghost town. Here,
he is now the resident hobo; everyone he knows
or knew has been recast. And the popping he hears
in his ears is just the sound of his joints, his pelvis, his hip,
splintering and fracturing under the strain

of playing buckaroo for so long. The final frame
accompanied by an overswelling score with untempered French horns

proclaims THE END, as if we did not already
know. We are led to worry about the end
of the world, but if truth be told, the world ends every
day; every day until all worlds end. And these,

these are the last lasts, the first firsts, and all the dithering
middles. And over here; at this end; ever so slightly, I lift
my head out of the dirt and ash. Without grudge or gripe
or quarrel, I gather. Vertebrae by tendon by cartilage, tablespoon
of blood and semen, milliliter of spit by tablespoon
of bile and sweat, bone ounce by organ ounce, skin gram by gram of

flesh. I pick up. And I start; I start again.

With the help of the weathervane,
the cockerel triumphant has found true north.

Proudly, he prepares his wake-up crow,
as the morning sun rises east.

"…from now on you will have the right to ask all the ghosts to tell you
the stories of their lives, and they will have to tell the truth about what
they've seen and touched and heard and loved and known in the
world…Your task will be to guide the ghosts…through the land of the
dead to the new opening out into the world. In exchange, they will tell
you their stories as a fair and just payment for this guidance."
"And we have the right to refuse to guide them if they lie, or if they
hold anything back, or if they have nothing to tell us. If they live in the
world, they *should* see and touch and hear and learn things."
— Philip Pullman, *The Amber Spyglass*

The Tattooed Man

answers all your questions.

Is it real?
No, it isn't. I have a medical condition where, in a narcoleptic state, I take medium-tipped felt pens and draw all over my body. My skin relishes the addictive drag of pen-tip to frayed nerves; it is a condition for which there is no support group at the YMCA. Science is still trying to discover what causes such unnatural urges. Scientists in the former Soviet bloc have suggested that it might be neurological snafus, crossed synapses; then communism fell and their research was abandoned in favor of new cutting-edge anti-aging cures.

What is it?
This one is a cocker spaniel playing in a lorry load of nettle flowers, see the skid marks? See the exhaust smoke? These are the helix strands of German ringworm. This is the only palm tree in No Man's Land, it also marks the exit and the turn-off to the superette. This, look closely, is a Belgravian peasant woman shucking oysters in the afternoon, see how much character there is in her face and hands and labor. This is the 104th angel embracing the 53rd demon, see their chipped wings? All their chipped wings? These are ice-cream trucks and this one is a celebrity chimpanzee, he's huge in Southeast Asia and Micronesia. This is a cream puff.

Does it hurt?
Only when the children point and laugh.

In the morning, I shall climb
onto the spiny back of another
20-hour flight, leaving
home, to go home, and already
missing home.

> "A home, the center where the three or four things
> That happen to a man do happen."
> — WH Auden, *Detective Story*

This night, he asked that the bedroom door
be left ajar. Such a ridiculous request,
not unheard of but who would.
The door should be shut
to keep the mosquitoes with all their bloody
borned diseases out. The warm calm blood of sleeping
bodies, so much more delicious than the chugging
blood of those awake in their bag of nerve and bones.
The door should be closed to keep
the air-conditioned cool air in.
Otherwise, what's the point of turning it on?
And those electric bills you'll get.

It is before sunrise. Outside,
the city's machinery shifting into first
gear quietly chugs and chuffs in the last
smolder of the streetlamps' sulfurous light.

In the flat, the light is fluorescent.

Dad is awake when I pull my wheelie-bag past
his open door.

"It's so early, go back to sleep," I said.
"I'm going to go now."

    "How can I sleep?" he said,
pointing to his belly, then lightly patting it.

I did not understand. I did not understand
what he was trying to say.

The brain had been misfiring his speech so much lately.

Think *Car*, but mouth say *Table*, and finger point *Window*.

Finger point *Belly*, mouth say *Awake*, Think: *What*...

do you say to your son when it might be the last time
you'll ever see him in what remains of your life?

What do you say to your father
when it is the last time you might see him alive?

And I said, "Just close your eyes. Go back to sleep.
   I'll turn off the lights for you."

The taxicab was waiting downstairs,
red tail-blinkers stuttering patiently.
By the time it gets me to the airport, the cracks
of the new day would have already started to poke
above the horizon of high-rises.

I switched off the lights.

And then, I left.

(Small Comfort)

The pot would be good if you want to keep on and keep up.
Otherwise, there is much better stuff in the hospital.

Sure, there are severe side effects: awful stenches,
dire organ failure, sleeplessness, psychosis, panic attacks,
and pain to replace pain, ache for ache.

And as the illness progresses,
the drugs will allow you to feel nothing. No pain.
Almost normal. If you didn't know otherwise.
Till right before the end.

At some point, there is this realization
that things are not going to get better.

There is no healing. None so, anymore.

There is a brick wall.
There is the edge of the cliff.
There is the on-coming train.

Unavoidably in your path. Head on,

and the only decision left is how hard
you want to put your foot down on the gas,
how you want to lay your heart down on the floor.

Oh honey, you'd be surprised
at the things you'd be able to do.
The things you're capable of
when the time comes.

Five blind men who have never before seen an elephant are led into a room where one is standing. Their task is to describe the elephant guided solely by touch.

The first man touches the elephant's leg.
"The animal is like a rubbery pole with stiff hairs," he says.

The second man touches the elephant's trunk.
"On the contrary, it is flexible, bendy, like octopus," he declares.

The third man touches the elephant's ear.
"No, the animal is really a thin leathery flapping wing," he concludes.

The fourth man steps into a huge steaming pile of elephant poo.
"What the fuck is this?" he screams.

All the touching and screaming annoys then frightens the elephant who starts panicking and bellowing. It stamps and kicks violently, indiscriminately; rearing up, it grabs anything in its path with its trunk and slams it onto the floor, stomping on it with all the might of its fear. One man's back has been snapped in five places from a kick, another three have been trampled, and resemble nothing more than a pile of bloody clothing and limbs. The splatter of blood, guts, flesh, hair and elephant poo speckles the room.

The fifth man begs, begs to be let out of the room. But the researchers watching behind the one-way glass window are merciless. There is a Guggenheim and a federal grant riding on this. And they have families to feed, inquisitive scientific minds to nourish.

Next week: Anaconda.

It cannot be this difficult. Really, it cannot. Scores of people lose their loved ones every day, and in far worse, far more horrifying circumstances: there are all sorts of warfare and race riots, murders and natural disasters, there are far more horrible diseases and unfortunate accidents, and this is not even mentioning the really freakish accidents like being trampled by runaway circus elephants, or being in the path of a spinout at the monster truck rally, or falling and being stuck in a volcanic crevasse.

I know I'm not the lowest nor will I ever be when all these other things are in dizzying play each and every single day. But of course, if we ever subscribed to that sort of comparison, then by right, there should be only one really miserable person in the world. And if that were the case, why isn't anyone – save the second most miserable person, he's exempt, we understand why he is hesitant to help – why aren't we all helping that one poor sod?

clotting, weight, brain fn, responsiveness,
neuromuscular control, surgery affect mental
(Options—) state? alt. to surgery? necessary?

over-chemo, over-medication.   reduce. how know
not working? how decide to stop. What factors shd govern
                                                      how not
work,
10 days->

Banking: Hong Leong (any account?) – yes? account still current
             Public –> Clinic Acct, Joint.

clinic mail redirect
car

what else?

The clinically piney smell of hospital grade
disinfectant makes any place seem a fair bit
sanitary, but a bog by any other name,
even one in Mount Elizabeth Hospital,

       is still and calm behind the hefty metal door.
I'm sitting on the loo with a syringe in hand,
a small vial of white power and one
of distilled water in the other.
The solution is mixed
to its precise injectible specifications.
I've been favoring the thigh
as the choice injection site of late.
My upper arms are too skinny and I just cannot bring
myself to stick my belly flab.

In the first few weeks, I studiously disinfected
the working area, and it would take hours
to work up the nerve to stick the needle into my flesh.
Never mind that the needle was splinter fine,
and subcutaneous was practically idiot-proof,
certainly miles easier than going for muscle or vein.
After a month, three months of this
routine, I'm sliding the cat over to one side
of my lap and doing my shot on the other, all in less
time than it takes to shake a tail feather
if I even had the energy to do that, much
less the moves.

Outside, my father is in radiation.
He will be done soon.
I will need to collect him, and bring him
upstairs to the third floor where a line
will be inserted into a vein in his arm
and he will receive a smattering of drugs,
some the same as what I'm counting on under

my skin, although his will be in much fiercer
neon concentrations.

The family assumes that I know
the particulars of side effects because I've done
my research, and I have.

I'll arrange for the car to send us home
where he will nap and I will nap
the afternoon away. We will wake
just before dinner time, bleary-eyed, every cell
in our bodies full of the wonders of modern
medicine, hungry and trying hard
to remember if any dreams came
at nap that afternoon.

It's good to take stock, collate the sum of discoveries, graph the teetering equation that governs what is known and what is believed, so to grasp the unfolding truths.

But it's better to dream of a field of pikake in bloom, better to talk to cats and dogs.

He was ill for so long, longer than the doctors expected, till the specialists and the consulting physicians did not know the next step, all they had to offer was bland platitudes and chirpy banter.

Of those diagnosed with the very same illness, half die within six months, 90 percent within nine. He held out for eighteen months.

Why did we think this was going to go on forever? Why did we buy that hospital bed rather than rent one? Or that wheelchair? Both of which have since been donated to some children's hospital. Why did we stock up on all those adult diapers? All those boxes have since been sent to some old-age home.

It was only a year and a half, but it seemed like a lifetime past and a lifetime to come. We forgot how he looked before this all started. We could not see when it would end. In spite of what we knew, we accepted that it was going to be like this from now on and we braced ourselves for the long haul.

Everyone knows the dying can cut out at any time. Why is he holding on? we asked ourselves and each other. He knows every thing has been squared off and away, all loose ends have been tied. There were no more obligations and responsibilities to speak of. All accounting had been taken and seen to.

Then I realized, it was *her*.

He was holding on for her. Because she wasn't yet ready. And she would never be. And all those years where I swore I would never become my parents came to tears one night in my room alone. The lull would be broken when she crashed through the door in a panic like I had never seen before. It was the first time in their forty years together that she had ever seen him vomit. And it scared her to witness it, especially under these circumstances. The hearty dinner of assam fish did not help matters, but he so enjoyed his food and it was a dinner with his younger siblings.

Those two, they have a language of their own, that not even my brother nor I could decipher. In the last weekend of his life, he was exceptionally lucid and present when all his friends came by busload to visit; and I knew, I just knew she had a hand in it. She would tell me later what she had done.

Scenes from the Oncologist's Office

"Chinese New Year is over already?"
The moment he said it, he knew he shouldn't have.
It was a clear sign that something was not quite right.
And it wouldn't be from that point forth.

She had booked time for mid-April
at the photo studio, determined to have
a nice professionally-taken family portrait,
framing and a choice of backdrop –
                         Chinese garden, waterfall, galaxy, cobalt blue, beige –
included in the package apparently.
It was now late in March
and she had no desire for the portrait
nor us the dread of it anymore.
All we could do was remember
what we used to look like
altogether.

                ★★★★★

She cannot bring herself to ask the doctors any questions,
blaming her nurse's training. It was all old-school:
the matron tells you what to do, and you do it,
no questioning, no discussing, efficient.
"Remember to ask," she reminds me in the waiting room.
And then, "You find out for me, okay? But please don't offend her."

She can't ask questions but she can answer them brilliantly.
In consultation, she speaks the same lingo as the doctors,
trading acronyms and abbreviations that make no sense to me,
but there's a lot of head nodding and *hmmm*ing;
I find reassurance in how none of the team of doctors
talks down or tries to dumb things down for her;
there, she is the superhero mom,
but once we leave the office, she's helpless
once again, incapable of ordering a taxi,
or using an ATM or cell phone.

★★★★★

The oncologist writes poems,
and is amazed at how patients
would bear their souls and even
their bodies to him.
Their own family members have never
seen them naked, he coos in wonder.

How many diseased bodies
does his meat-grinder of a muse need
as grist for his lovely and sensitive poems
that *understand* and *reveal* such jeweled truths?

Poetic truths, it is universally known,
last longer than a spouse's sorrow,
a family's grief.

★★★★★

"So you're the son in the U.S.? They like to ask a lot of questions there."

★★★★★

Proudly displayed on the wall,
a framed press clipping, where
in an interview, the oncologist reveals
that if she were to do it all over again,
she would chose to be an engineer.

★★★★★

My mother and my brother have a row in the oncologist's waiting room.
Something about her wanting to pay with her credit card.
And he insisting that she should not rack up debt, not at this time.
His civil service insurance will cover it, he says.
But you need to save it up for your own family, she says.
Now, mother and brother are doing what theater folk call "using the space."

And these are not patients patiently waiting for the doctor, they are an
   unwilling captive audience.
I wheel my dad to the far corner where we pretend we do not know
   these two.
As she has done for thirty-five years, she wants Dad to lay down her law.
Don't get me involved, he says, and he picks up the newspaper lying there.
It's the "Life" section, the article is on this season's must-have handbags,
   but he pretends to peruse it thoughtfully anyway.
I'm embarrassed and wondering how long does it take to run a bill.
She'll get her way, he'll fume, they'll make up by lunchtime, tomorrow
   breakfast at the most.
Dad puts the paper down and leans back, he looks up at me bemused.
We'll meet you in the lobby, I say; I wheel him out the door.
En route to the elevator, he makes an odd throaty sound.
Did he choke? Is it the dry air in the building?
Wait, that was a chuckle. That was most definitely a chuckle.
And it sounds right, good even.

That tired old joke about cockroaches and Cher
being all that's left, how he found it so amusing
as if it were the first time he had heard it.
He aligned not with the invincibility,
but the tenacity; how many times
did he teeter on the brink, to have done
all the goodbyes only to get stuck
in the revolving door and then

                            hello again,
my friend.

And he was, somehow
        and by what byways.

In the white water of the first wave,
he was thrown (threw himself?)
into a raft, undertowed
by this haunted city's wreck and rips.

      "What garment would you wear at the end of the world?"

The strain in him,
ever replicating its genetic code
since, had lineage to

        the originating one, the Alpha.
        That vile organism,

the shadow of so much annihilated in its wake,
monstrous in its sleeplessness and slaughter.

Now, after working its persistent
ruin for thirty years
it will live for thirty-odd more
days past the wreckage, then it will
die in earth;

sooner

if there's cremation,
where it's fire for flame,

right there and then.

And we will be clothed in the robes of queens and princes.

(for Thomas Avena)

(Snakes, Ladders)

Feet on Square One, eyes towards One Hundred, skipping on this path littered with snakes and ladders. Oh, why didn't I bring my bamboo snake-whacker? Why didn't I wear my non-slip climbing soles?

It's Americans mostly I've found who call the game "Chutes & Ladders." Which just seems oddly inaccurate. A chute evokes the image of the dumpyard where to-be abandoned babies wrapped in swaddling clothes are chucked down. A chute denotes one direction and that direction is down. Does anyone, has anyone, ever chuted upwards?

"Snakes & Ladders," now that makes sense. The ladder holds in itself the same perils as the snake. The risk taken climbing up — your footing may slip through the rungs, the ladder may slip off its grips, the props might fail — equal the risk sliding down on snakes.

Ladders in play, immediately creates an ill spot. Never mind you've been down that path all your life, thrice a day, trusting in your safe return. Enter Ladder. Walk under, and who knows what. And snakes, Lucifer, fall of Eden, evil slither, fangy poison, cursed by God.

Even though I never thought of the snakes in the game as poisonous. Too colorful with diamante patterns to really be poisonous, the best I'd entertain would be faux-poison, like a mosquito bite. Something that would cause great itchiness and sin. So much as to just be really slippery, possibly aided by some kind of mucus secretion.

Once, my brother and I played a game of no-rules, no-holds Snakes and Ladders governed by two dice. You could climb up the back of a snake as much as fall down a ladder. Snake and Ladder could intersect creating an up-down-side-slashing luge. You could go, end up almost anywhere.

We laughed like mad and the game lasted for more then five hours, a game without end it seemed, a game that we would never tire of. Until a lucky toss of the dice: scramble up a snake, up a ladder, down another, space, space, up a snake, up a ladder and a one, two, three, four, exactly on Home: the imaginary square 101, the single step off the board, out of the game.

How do we go from tomb to tumor? You are.
Two of you if the Commonwealth is involved.

How do you go from tomb to tomb in French? Water.

> "Let me weep. It is no shame
> Weeping men are good…
> Let me weep. Tears give life to dust.
> Already it is greening."
> — Johann Wolfgang Goethe, *West-Eastern Divan*

It has been a long and difficult year
and nothing in my life has prepared me
for how to cope with it.

Wherever life exists,
there is inconsistency,
there is division and strife;

we make progress,
we find clarity
by facing conflict.

All the while hoping it doesn't lead
to a simple and mindless conclusion.

Hoping that it will dispute the lie
that life is pointless and mean;

that life is not colored by a chasming lack
and not colored by silence,
and certainly not by babble or clattering idiots,

but by such abundance, something good,
something with dignity, some measure
that cannot be destroyed by indifference,
disaster, politics, illness, and tragedy.

Something that does not die
against the daily death.

My great fear is that I do not know
what happiness actually is. I'm afraid
I will become one of those people
who gets used to something
and calls it

'happiness' simply
because I cannot imagine
                              anything else.

And snakes, of course.

That, snakes and giant hairy killer spiders.

What is particularly horrifying
would be if a snake should slither in here right now,
with giant hairy spiders on its back.
Each of the spiders would be wearing a hockey mask
and wielding a chainsaw.

Don't laugh,
spiders have eight legs:
they can comfortably hold onto the snake,
hold a hockey mask in place since the elastic band
clearly won't fit around their little nippy heads,
hold a chainsaw, and still
have five free appendages to waggle at me,
mocking me for not knowing happiness.

W.W.J.K.

Who Would Jesus Kill?

"…may cause patient to develop mood or behavioral problems. These can include irritability (getting easily upset) and depression (feeling low, feeling bad about yourself, or feeling hopeless). Some patients may have aggressive behavior. Some patients think about hurting or killing themselves or other people and some have killed (suicide) or hurt themselves or others… Certain symptoms like severe stomach pain may mean that your internal organs are damaged."
— *Insert of a Schering Corporation pharmaceutical drug package*

I was the wallflower at all the rain dances.

Oh, how violetly warm and dry it has been.

Now they're playing my favorite slow jam.

Oh, why did I not get new insoles for those Red Shoes?

(Happiness)

When it first appeared on the scene
all across Old Europe, it was used
to wish luck upon,
as if, and is it not?
based on an outlaw's luck.
Except for the Welsh
who traded luck for smarts.
      Did wisdom beget happy
      or is it happier to be wise?
It took half a century
before it absorbed gladness.
Given life expectancies at that time,
so many of the lucky and the wise died
not knowing the giggles.
But still, it took another 190 years
before its condition was recorded.
And another 406 years before it
was extended to clams.
Prior to that, clams and other bivalves
were nothing if not sullen and tasty.

      Waking with the one you love.
      The sleeping and purring cat in bed.
      Wonderment shared with little nieces and nephews.
      A good prayer. A good book.
      A meal with friends.
      A day without care or bother.
      Remission.

Happiness is never overrated.

The instructions,
laid out on the photocopied page given to us,
seemed simple enough.

      Monday 9 a.m. Sharp.
      Bring your own urn. (Minimum Volume: 2 liters).

All weekend: Is this an urn or a vase?
                   Melamine or porcelain?
                   Big enough? Too big?
                   Plain or motifed with flowers? or script or koi?
                   Display or transport only?

The final choice: A soup tureen,
more tall than rounded, tastefully Oriental
in porcelain blues and whites.

Even if we came empty-handed, urn undecided,
on Monday morning, we still could have hastily
purchased one from all those being sold
out of the backs of cars and vans in the parking lot.

In the waiting room, the attendant brings in
a blue plastic pail. He pours the contents out
on the small table we are gathered around.

Ash, thick ropes of dust,
the color of heavily-milked tea.

And bones. Chips and chunks,
a smattering of chalky white.
If we didn't know different,
we could mistake these for pieces
of coral, picked illegally off the reefs.
Certainly not what is left
on the crematorium oven floor.

They say that the average person
cremates into six, maybe eight, pounds.
In the old days, some even believed
that the human soul weighed 21 grams.

He was a small man, athletic,
but short, just five feet tall
and not more than 130 pounds tops.
Born during the Japanese Occupation,
we were always told,

> not enough food, stunted growth.

How much does this pile
of ash and bones in front of me
weigh? Metric or imperial,
I have no reference to gauge.

Use your hands, the attendant advises.
He points to the sink, *you can wash up later.*

We scoop into the dusty pile
with both hands, one cupped hand, fistful,
transferring it to the urn.

> *Ashes to ashes, dust to dust.*
> We've heard it so often said.
> We forget it was meant literally.

Dust it may be,
that it can so easily be blown away
by a slight breeze from a carelessly left
open window, swept away with a duster,
but dust it is that bears the weight
of a crumpled heart, the assumed dream
of an old-age spent together now irrecoverable.

Ash it is that is diminution
of a shared life:
          intimate, paternal, civic.

Ash and dust it will be
          that is burdened on those
whose hands it covers.

There is one piece, embedded
into what must have been his skull,
a little knot of surgical twine,
one of the stitches that sought
to hold skullpiece to skullpiece.

This knot should have easily disintegrated
in the rapid bursts of the crematorium fires.

Day after day,
          one after another,
eight hours a day,
          five days a week,

the unmerciful fires produce
these piles of brittle bone & dust & ash,
how did this little silly bit survive?

What will the fishes think of it?
Will they mistake it for coral?

Grief comes in waves,
high tide, low tide, till it's done.
Time harbors, sets its breakers and fail-safes
but grief comes in such waves;
set adrift, eyeshot far from tomb and grave
still, the floods flash ash to ashes to dust
Grief comes in lapping waves
high tide, low tide, never done.

In the day, we take naps wherever we can find the space, we lie with a t-shirt or a towel over our faces to block out the light and noise and steal a nap wherever opportunity allows. In the night, we pull together the sofa cushions to make a bed, run downstairs to the car to bring up the sleeping bags, and we pack five, six to a room, lying side by side in efficient lots. Just watch where you're stepping if you need to go to the toilet in the night, we say to each other. Sometimes we think this is funny and we laugh, most times, we are too tired to laugh. Or cry. Or dream. We plunge into deep sleep the moment the lights go out, or when we lay horizontal, even if we meant to lie down for just mere seconds. We drop into a bottomless sleep the moment we are still. Dreamless, we don't feel the night go by, the hours pass, and the next thing we know, it's sunrise, it's morning. In the morning, the ones on the night watch come back in to get some sleep. Sometimes, they don't come back up, preferring to just sleep on the bench downstairs.

In the morning, we wait patiently for the bathroom to become available. There are only two bathrooms, one in the master bedroom and one in the kitchen. It's first come, first served unless there is a full bladder emergency, or one of the kids needs to use the bathroom. In the morning we plot out the activities for the day, we lay out the responsibilities and we take on what we can, what we must. We try to help each other out whenever we can.

We find out who's staying for lunch, we figure out how many packets of food to buy from the market, and who will go to do this. Most of all, we just need to be around, to receive the wreaths, to sign for deliveries. And to make sure strangers don't steal anything since it's all laid out in the open, but no one will, of course, the taint of death makes it all taboo, no object — no matter how valuable — is worth that sort of risk, of defiling the consecrated.

We wanted to have the wake in the void deck of the apartment building. Someone else had their wake there just a week before. Every wake you saw in passing always used the void deck. But then, as permits go, someone else had done so illegally, sans permit. No, you have to use the common area, the permits insisted. This requires us to move all arrangements around the adjoining blocks of flats, past the playground, away from the parking garage, in full view of all the blocks of flats. Here, the funeral home contractors set up their tent, folding tables and chairs, icebox filled with packs of drinks and bottled water, standing fans, and everything else we will need: pens, writing paper, safety pins, small squares of black, blue, white cloth. They will come by every morning and evening to replenish supplies.

It is also where the coffin is laid.

We need to be around to greet visitors. They start coming in the late morning. They come all afternoon and all through the night even. Church members, business colleagues, friends from school and college, and of course, relatives. Most of them we have never seen before, have no idea who they are. We will look in the condolence book later. "Mountain Top Uncle's Son." "Pig Dog Family Relatives." Or they will tell us. "The last time I saw your father was at his wedding." "The last time I saw you, you were just a baby; and you, you weren't even born yet."

Little by little, with or without their help, with the help of an assortment of aunts and uncles and their encyclopedic knowledge of births and marriages, we'll figure out how these visitors are related to us. Grandma's Father's Sixth Uncle's Third Daughter's Youngest Son. Fourth Granduncle's Youngest Daughter who's married to Uncle Meng's Second Son, Their Son was in School with Your Cousin, This is His Son. The ones who know for sure off the backs of their hands, the grandmothers, have all passed away a year ago. Which is just as well, even though we miss their sensible natures and their down-to-earth ways of getting by, since we suspect that this would surely break them down, wreck them more than anything else in their long lives, but surely we under-estimate their mettle.

In the afternoon, we sit around the dining room table, the ceiling fan on its highest setting, or downstairs in the tented area with all the standing floor fans at full blast. Inevitably someone would have bought more food, someone would cook some more, or some well-wishers would bring a Tupperware of something or another. There is always food, too much food, but by the evening, there is never any. And in the evening, we will need to find out who's staying for dinner, how much food to order from the neighboring hawker centers and who will go get it.

But in the afternoon, all day, we sit and eat and talk. We tell stories we've told before. We tell stories we've heard before, we've heard them many times before, but still we tell them and we listen to them as if it were the very first time we have told them or heard them. And every time someone else tells a story we already know, we find a new story we haven't yet heard. We compare versions of the same story. We discover different stories to what we already know. Of course, all the stories involve the one who isn't here.

Around the table talking story, suddenly so much makes sense, so much becomes clearer, comes into sharper focus, the gaps get filled. I hear for the first time how all my aunts received secondary education, college even, over the objections of my grandfather, who felt it a waste to educate girls: it was he who argued for weeks, took on a hunger strike until the old man relented. I hear for the first time how he helped his younger brother cram for his university entrance exam. I find out even more about his brief political career. All I remembered was his election poster, and his emblem, a bicycle, plastered all around town on lampposts, bus stops, sides of buildings, as was the style of campaigning at the time. This time I learned what a fine orator he was, speaking off the cuff at rallies, calling on his education of the Chinese classics; I learned of his party's desertion; and I learned of the kidnap threats made on my brother and me. I never knew why there were so many people always around us, never leaving us alone during our preschool years.

I learned about the financial deals he made, loans cosigned to help his younger brother, all done on his part on a handshake and on someone's word of honor. And of course, how certain "partners" had cut out and left him holding the bag. I learned about the time the Tongs' salted fish goods store burned down and how, during his mid-morning tea break, he had gone to them quietly and offered a substantial loan without interest or deadlines to help them rebuild. Before his illness, every alternate Wednesday was cheap movie night with the Tongs. It was on holiday with the Tongs when he bought the last Christmas present he ever gave me, a serving set just like the ones they use at Ah-Soon's, the coffee shop where we would go for coffee whenever I was home.

In the late afternoon, someone will take the kids to the playground and watch over them as they play. Then, we will wash up and get dressed and get ready for the evening services. Earlier in the day, we walk out to the main road and tie strips of black ribbon to lampposts, street signs and guard railings, leading all the way in to the correct block and the correct parking lot. The newspapers had printed an incorrect address and then there was the confusion between the proper street address and the more direct route, obtained by cutting across the development. Somehow, this trail of black ribbon is understood, and well-wishers find their way. The ribbons may have blown away or been removed by street-sweepers and we will need to do this again the next day.

In the evening, the tables are folded up and the chairs are laid out in rows. We take our places for the evening's services. We will meet with visitors until past midnight. And then someone will stay up all night. The others will find a place to sleep. Someone might wake up before sunrise and join the one sitting up all night.

We will do this every day until the cortege leaves for the cremation. Then we will pick up the ashes, get the papers sorted out, and fly home. There, we will have another wake and another service, one for those who could not travel, for his patients and for his hometown friends, acquaintances and associates.

But today at the service, we are seated in the front row. The funeral home has prepared a large framed photo of him from the photo we have provided them. He looks so dashing, so healthy, so different from how we've seen him daily for the last year, from how he's lying there. Is this what he used to look like? Had we forgotten how he used to look? Then I notice it. I lean over and tell my mom, and then my brother. The funeral home had taken liberties in giving him a fuller head of hair. They had graciously photoshopped and felt-tip penned a plumpness and volume to his hairline. And we can't help ourselves. We start giggling and laughing, laughing and giggling, if only because we've cried so much, each in private, each in our own bewilderment, that we don't think we can cry anymore.

It seemed the simplest of tasks, this last one.
To find a boat to bring us out to sea for the scattering.
But the specter of death makes this tricky amongst the fisherfolk.
We find someone so poor that a chance at income
trumps any superstition.
We set out early morning.
To curb the rising seasickness, focus on the horizon.
Or sit in front of the boat, away from the engine.
The kerosene engine burns and fumes its nauseating smoke.

   Dad used to be such an avid fisherman.
   He once took us deep-sea fishing, and I was never seasick.
   That pastime fell to the side early on.
   Golfing sank its tender putting hook in.

The boat goes by the Royal Kuantan Golf Course.
Soon, we will be able to see their condo as well.

   The reason he bought the condo was the view of the sea.
   The monsoon savage sea was something to behold.

The sea starts to get really choppy now, and we decide to stop.
Mom goes first; then my brother and I.
Then his brothers and sisters.
Handful by handful, each.
Each dip into the burnished emerald of the South China Sea.
The ash expands in a murky cloud as it sinks.
The few pieces of porous bone bring up bubbles as they sink.
Then we tell the fisherman to head back.
It is mid-morning by now.
The mouth of the river is clogged with refuse and sewage.
The aunts are leaning over the edge of the boat vomiting.
They will continue vomiting even after we are on land.
I'm feeling mighty queasy myself.
But I inhale the burning kerosene and the raw sewage in easy gulps.
I've just scattered what's left of my father to the tide.
I want my unsettling gut to match my unsettling landscape.

The four leather golf bags, wrapped up in white plastic trashbags against the dust and sun, hang their shrouded club heavy heads like skulking nuns in the corner.

When awoken sweating from the heat in the middle of the night during a revolving brown-out, they might be hooded mynahs mourning in the company of monks.

Narrowing

Less than a month after they tore down the freeway overpass, disused
since the earthquake, they're tearing down the projects across the street
with cranes and wrecking balls, earthmoving equipment; all sorts of
heavy iron machinery boom, making the entire building shake, the
windows rattle and hum, the panes vibrate like tuning forks in all their
termite-cracked minor flats; they've unleashed something into the air,
those old buildings are like sporebags, crack them and next you know,
things are growing out of *stuff*, and voila! you have sourdough and some
sort of yeasty new beer, but my respiratory passages can't bear this new
air much more, I've tried over-the-counters and two different
prescription inhalers and still, it's all snot and tissues, drips and atissue,
laboriously breathing through the mouth, which will only lead to a sinus
infection; pity, it's so nice out, spring weather in the middle of fall, and
I want to go look for some discarded drawers at the secondhand thrift
store; I like that aesthetic though at times I feel the pangs of wanting and
needing more grown-up furniture, but how can anyone pass up the
drama of a thrift store, a place so rife with heartbreak, where the
remnants of a past era of living — stuff that was once the newest of the
latest, the must-own fad, the pride and joy of a home — find refuge; in
primary school, we were assigned English compositions where we had to
write the 'autobiography' of an inanimate object, like a pen or a kite or a
pair of shoes, and I don't remember any of the heroes of those accounts
ever ending up in a thrift store; I can see the one regret of not living a
long time is the amusement of walking into a thrift store at a point in
the future, to see it filled to the rafters (or will they have done away with
rafters by then?) with all the Philippe Starck and Alessi crap, bottle-
openers made to look like toadstools, chairs made to seat gray alien butts,
all that hyper-designed stuff all for under a buck; but the fatigue is
getting the better of me, my options are to fight and not let it get the
upper hand, because once you're left with the lower hand, you'll be
forever sifting dirt, or I can just give in graciously, the breathing situation
is not helping and the days are getting shorter ever so progressively, but
what that really means is daylight shortens, days are always twenty-four
hours, but that's moot, since I don't have quite as many good hours in a
day as I once had; just as the daylight shortens, as day shortens, so life
narrows, which I never in my wildest thought it would; as a young man

starting out in the world, I expected life to expand in roiling curlicues, like how gases fill a space or how smoke talks to clouds, but our 'ways' set in, comfort levels peak, tastes and preferences solidify, tolerance and curiosity harden, each decision made or deferred shuts down more doors than I knew even existed, bit by bit, the six-lane highway leads to a single rural lane, a cow walking this gauntlet would wonder if it leads to a branding, a feed trough or the abattoir, sometimes, it might even lead to a grassy meadow but the cow doesn't know or expect that; the building stops rumbling and quaking as if in awe of the encroaching sunset; sometimes, usually during the good hours of my day, I understand that there are those who take a certain joy in this narrowing.

I've read somewhere
that the Icelandic language has recognized 27 words for ghosts.
And that the Albanian has 17 for moustache.
And that in Japanese, the 'I' of a child and the 'I' of an adult
are different words.

> "Papa, I saw a spookie with a handlebar moustache."
> "I don't think so, little one, that spirit's got a zapata."

I was once told the name,
which I've since forgotten,
of the groove found in corduroy. Last
year, three thousand five hundred new words were added
to the Oxford English Dictionary.

Given the gargantuan heft and sheer depth of each
and all the language in this world, committed
to page, throat, hands –
have some pity on the concierge,
the front desk and staff at the Hotel Babel –
how do words fail so unspeakably
in the boxcutter grip of grief?

How many inexpressible sadnesses weigh
against how many indescribable happinesses?

An equal measure of elephants in one
weighing pan against toenails in the other.

What is this
ache's native tongue?

Why can I not name all
that I don't know how to ask for?
Trying to is like asking
a heathen to swear on a stack of bibles.
Easier to wipe the slate,
shake the Etch-a-Sketch.

I have no wish to forget
my grief nor be healed of it.
There is room in my heart
and head and gut. There is enough room
too for silence. They may even be
room some day
for stillness.

You will be shocked
at how much this world can grace.
And how little of that
will ever salt your tongue
or find its way into your lexicon.

There should be enough language in our lifetime
to ask for God.

There should be words enough
to tame our hearts,

and to beg it,
stay.

Two days after my dad's funeral,
I am playing with my three-year-old niece.
She has just kicked me out of the tea party,
exiled to the sofa to observe only,
no pretend finger foods for Uncle.
Mid-party, she picks up her Elmo cell-phone.
"Hello," I hear her say into the bright red mouthpiece,
"No, Kong-kong is not at home now; he's in heaven,
okay, goodbye." She stops and considers for a while,
then she allows me back into the tea party.
But only if I take sensible bites of the fish sandwiches
she has prepared, and sensible sips from the little teacup.

That I can do.

The other night, I dreamt of a father who lasted forever.

I loved him and I loathed him. I scorned his gifts.
I disdained him and I wanted him.
I wanted him to see me, yet I lurked in the dark.
I respected him and feared him.
I saw his gold, I saw his shit, I sold his gold and shoveled his shit.
I stole his shirts, his car, his fillings.
He caned me, belted me; I was naughty, a disciplined child.
I broke his bones, and then his spirit. I fed him and clothed him.
I held him to my breath.
He was comfort to my terror, I lived in such mighty abandoning waves.
He soothed my homesickness; he was my home, I his sick.
I counted his pills, prepared his shot. He did not complain. I bitched like
    mad.
He never shed a single tear, even as I filled rooms with mine.
I slept fetal by his side, dreamt his dreams.
I stoned his dreams. Oh what mighty boulders I flung at his pebbly
    dreams.
He gave me all the food that money could buy.
He gave me an ulcer no money in the world would look at.
I made him presents of my youthful blame, such lovely bitter nuggets.
I obeyed him and I trusted him. He saw to it that I always did.
I showed him the rose that had bloomed in the garden and he showed
    me the hole where we could bury the cat.
I understood his ways. I prayed with him, for him, around him. And
    when he wasn't looking, I prayed for someone else.
He took the chip-shot off my shoulder, I took the chips out of his old
    block.
He hid my ugly scars and I built us a house of cards, all aces, sevens,
    & jokers.
I shook the dust off his wings, hoping he would fly and show me how;
    he took the sleep out of my heart.
This time I would be the one who went away, the one everyone counted on
    who didn't stay.

In this dream of the father that lasted forever,
my dad forgave me, and this time, I learned to forgive myself.

My rage then ceased to need a name.

A dream only becomes one
            when you wake up.

I wake up.
I am lying in rubble.
Everything is mud.
My homes have become holes.
I have no strength to sit up.
I have no shovel.

Me and My Helper Monkey

It has come to this at last. My health is on the blink,
and I am informed that I cannot qualify for all the super
home health services my city offers. But do I really want
the volunteer from the health agency, some stranger working off
his multitude of parking tickets while squaring out his karma?
Who's got time or push to strap down the stereo, hide all valuables
and imported beer, the good CDs and books?
                                            No, what I really want
is simply, a helper monkey. A gamely gibbon, or a plucky baboon.
Even an agreeable howler monkey. But most of all, a nice fuzzy
spider monkey. Certainly not chimpanzees, they're too focused on
their showbiz careers to care about anyone else. And certainly not
Orangutans or Gorillas, because they shed like fuckers
and are constantly doped up on dried coconut husks. No. I shall
have a lovely Spider Monkey with a wizened beard, preferably,
and I shall call my helper monkey, Steve.

Oh what grand times Steve, My Helper Monkey, and I will have.
His chores are to retrieve the mail from the down the stairs,
scoop the cat poop and change the cat litter, wash the dishes,
collect my laundry from the wash-and-fold, buy Diet Coke
and Ben & Jerry's from the corner grocery, and return my DVDs
to the local neighborhood video store. With Steve, My Helper Monkey,
I will no longer suffer any nonsense from the surly clerks
at the video store. No more will they over-deduct credits
from my card, charge me nonexistent late fees and accidentally lose
the 10-rental credit I paid for. With one screeching fang-baring snarl
and its ensuing spray of saliva possibly tainted with Ebola, Steve,
My Helper Monkey, will make things right again at that Evil Hole.
I will make Steve, My Helper Monkey, a small coin pouch that he wears
strapped across his monkey chest like a Prada shoulder bag.
He will be the envy of all the other helper monkeys; lesser monkeys
with their Kaiser fanny packs cannot even bear to look at him.

I will remind Steve, My Helper Monkey, not to swing so carefree
from the phone wires. Reminding him of one particular monkey

I once knew long ago in my childhood. That little monkey was named
Foo, and he belonged to my neighbor, the loud-mouthed, wife-beating,
Doberman-rearing lawyer Joseph Aw. Foo was such a delightful
little monkey. Every morning, while the Dobermans were eating
their vittles, he would swing on over to our kitchen window
and just hang there. Mom would feed him small cut-up pieces of fruit.
Even my stern Dad was won; "so bloody cute," Dad clucked,
and gave him a piece of buttered toast topped with a generous lump
of orange marmalade. Foo was a happy monkey, swinging around
the neighborhood, being fed by his legion of admirers, talking
to the macaws in the trees, singing happy songs with family dogs
and cats. But one day, the poor thing was swinging on the phone wires
and he made a connection, positive to negative. It was a hotline
1-800-Collect Call to the Monkey God, who accepted the charges.
Poor Foo was burned to a little crispy thing. His body was stuck
to the phone wire and as much as Mrs. Aw tried to knock it down,
first using a long pole, then eventually, by throwing sneakers at it,
the charred body stayed stuck to the phone wires and so she left it.
Foo hung on to those wires for months, a memorial to his loving
carefree monkey days, until his body decomposed and fell off.
His body fell off but his arms still clung to the phone wire
like notes on a music score, a sharp note held on by a cracking jazz
musician. Eventually, those flea-infested arms that would hold you
so lovingly around your neck decomposed and fell off too; now all
that was left were his fingers, mere knuckles stuck to the wire.
Steve, My Helper Monkey looks at me, his monkey eyes fearfully wide
and quivering with tears; in his high-pitched monkey screech,
he promises that he will be careful.

With Steve, My Helper Monkey, in my life, I can finally go
to Rainbow Grocery to buy bulk rice. At the prices they charge,
you would think they would get one of the stoned hippie employees
to park his damn bicycle, and come inside to help pick the weevils out
of the grain. That is all moot, now that I have Steve, My Helper Monkey,
with me. With his nimble fingers, and his blood memory of picking nits
whilst grooming assorted siblings and cousins, sorting the weevils
out of a sack of rice is no problem. We do this chore together,
spreading the sack's contents out on the kitchen table. Steve moves

fast, and more than occasionally, I have to stop and chastise him
when he can't resist eating the crunchy weevils so packed
with beta-proteins. "Spit it out!" I scold, holding my palm out
and Steve, My Helper Monkey, sheepishly pulls out the weevil
he has put into his mouth. I know it is hard for any monkey to resist
this fat protein snack, but these aren't weevils you find in a forest,
these are vegan co-op grocery weevils, who know what carcinogens
or cooties they harbor. Sometimes I pretend to look the other way;
sometimes, Steve, My Helper Monkey, is just too fast, slamming
the weevils into his mouth and chewing them down before I notice.
Inevitably, Steve, My Helper Monkey, comes to me a day or two later,
looking all piteous pointing to his mouth. A weevil is stuck
between his teeth. "Serves you right!" I scold again, but he and I
both know that I will eventually floss his teeth for him.
While sorting rice, Steve, My Helper Monkey, and I realize our bond,
we realize how truly alone we are in this world. My family
and homeland so far away and I somewhat disconnected from them;
and he, his jungle razed to the ground so the 12th largest
football stadium in the world could be built; where in the off-season,
Rainforest Benefit concerts are held, featuring Sting who assembles
a group of malnourished underprivileged Amazonian Indians as his
back-up singers. Steve, My Helper Monkey, is amazed
how the natives managed to work their lip-plates around
the difficult consonants of all those annoying Police songs.
He was so sure those lip-plates would come dislodged during "Roxanne."

Every day when the weather is good, Steve, My Helper Monkey, and I
go for little walks in the neighborhood. He swings merrily from
lamppost to treetop to traffic sign above me. Cute boys with dogs will
stop to check us out and give me their phone numbers. Life with Steve,
My Helper Monkey, is not all hunky-dory lovely walkies. One time walking,
we passed the Pier One Imports. And something snapped:
Steve, My Helper Monkey, suddenly went berserk, as if a primal force
had possessed him. He whipped off his new Kate Spade backpack,
and dashed into the store, howling and heading straight for the Fall
wicker collection. He climbed into each and every wicker basket
and hamper on display, crying and snarling and smearing handfuls
of his feces all over the wicker coasters, lampshades, and placemats.
It was awful. But none more than the time I discovered strange oily

smears on my flatbed scanner. Then wiry dry hairs stuck
to my computer keyboard. Steve, My Helper Monkey, was having
an Internet affair with Julie, a helper monkey in Wisconsin,
who was assigned to a young woman with MS. Late at night,
Steve, My Helper Monkey, would scan dirty dirty pictures
of his glowing monkey ass in heat and e-mail them to Julie.
I had to let the affair run its course. I know the pain of love,
and I know the greater pain of not loving. Then,
Julie's guardian was miraculously healed by Pastor Benny Hinn
on his evangelical tour of the Great Lakes. Julie was gone.
Just like that. Poor Steve. How he pined. So much so that he lay
on the futon, unable to move or groom or scratch, struggling to breathe
and to make sense of life and love in all its baffling permutations.
The roles were then reversed. It was I who had to care for him.
In his weakened state, in what we all thought might be his final
night, Steve, My Helper Monkey, reaches for the Palm Pilot
with his prehensile tail and slowing types a message to me. *Steve.*
Want. Ba Na. He is too weak to continue but our bond has become such
that I know exactly what he wants.

     I bake him Banana Nut Bread
topped with a thick cream cheese frosting and a generous sprinkling of weevils.
    Like all broken hearts, even monkey ones,
Steve, My Helper Monkey's heart mends and we return to our daily grind
and grinding, we resume our little lives so filled with trifles
and cheers; until the turning of that day when my health
irrevocably fails. Here in my final days, Steve, My Helper Monkey
performs his grandest gestures. He knows it is my vain and miscarried
dream, my secret desire, to grow into being the sort of man
who can get away with a name like Scooter, T-Bone, Boomer or Clifford.
In my dying moments, Steve My Helper Monkey takes the Epson Label Maker,
which he bought online at Overstock.com, he just could not resist
the free shipping, no monkey can, and he types those names out
one by one, in every font and size, on every last label.
He gently sticks each label, one by one, to my fevered forehead.
Then, perplexed as to why my body is so cold and stiff, he swings over
to The Gap and shoplifts a woolly sweater which he tries to put on me.
But rigor mortis makes that a difficult task, even for such a clever
monkey, so at my wake, Steve, My Helper Monkey, attentively sits
by my coffin and makes sure the sweater is draped over me at all times.

He is confused, hysterical when I am shoved into the crematorium,
and desperately grabs hold of my foot to stop me from sliding
into the flames. But the heat and the gas burners singe his fur
and he lets the foot go and runs off into the trees screaming
holy terror, anguished that he didn't hold on tighter
or with all five limbs.

    At my grave, Steve, My Helper Monkey, sits
on my headstone waiting for me to come back, and go rice-sorting
with him, to help him download monkey porn. Like Grey Friar's Bobby,
Steve, My Helper Monkey, sits on my headstone diligently waiting.
Well-wishers bring him small plates of food, which he nibbles from,
but he never leaves his spot. Nothing would make him move from that
one spot, not rainstorms nor hail, not drive-bys nor parades;
mating seasons come and go and his monkey ass glows red then back
to brown until it stops glowing altogether. The back of my headstone
is streaked with syrupy monkey pee, and positively covered
in monkey poo. Still, Steve, My Helper Monkey, waits. Until
one Spring day, 17 years later, overcome with exhaustion and old-age
and sadness, Steve, My Helper Monkey, looks up into the trees
and in the highest branches, he sees me sitting with Julie,
I'm holding a Tupperware bursting with banana nut bread, frosted
with cream cheese and weevils. Steve, My Helper Monkey, sighs, quietly
screeches his monkey screech, then he tips over and dies.

He is buried in a plot a few feet away from me.
A small monument is erected in honor of my helper monkey.
His coin pouch is bronzed. Every year, thousands of seeing-eye dogs
and helper monkeys make the pilgrimage to his grave. They pee
and rub their hindquarters against the marble monument
to my dear helper monkey.

    And in a jungle somewhere so deep
that no one has yet discovered, a tree grows, a new species
whose flowers blossom and produce a fruit that tastes not unlike
banana nut bread frosted with cream cheese. Weevils are naturally
drawn to that fruit. A whole wilderness of monkeys live in that tree,
not realizing that in those fruit lies the miracle serum
that can cure all human illness.

He realized that war interrupted his dreaming;

In the last scene of the dream,

I lift up my teacup, a black spider no bigger than a press-on nail lies belly-up in a puddle of unsweetened Earl Grey, its eight legs curled oh-so symmetrical hugging its slightly furry abdomen. In the whiff of bergamot, I mistake it for star anise.

The air hangs thick with dust, I walk into my apartment but it is so much brighter indoors. My pupils constrict so blood-worn I cannot see. My throat begins to swell, I cannot breathe. I put my fingers into my throat to pry an air passage but instead, I choke on them.

The two backpacks I am carrying, one slung over each arm, grow increasingly heavy, I recognize the dark dense of the rolling blackout, I cannot move, my eyes unaccustomed. There is a scuffle at the gas station down the block, someone menacing runs by me, someone is thrown across the hood of his car.

I tell Angela Lansbury, "Trained seals only know how to perform in one way."

The nurse intercepts me in the stairwell and swabs the crook of my arm with alcohol, then draws my blood with a very long very curved needle, attached by a sip-thin hose to a machine. From the belly of that machine, a conveyor belt produces a steady output of hamburgers and 3-tiered chocolate cupcakes.

The best man at the wedding takes the second best dining chair out into the hallway and jumps up and down on it.

A tin of mashed sardines in tomato sauce, sliced hard-boiled eggs, on soft white bread. Now I am generously sprinkling the open-faced sandwich with capsules of an indeterminate medicine.

I watch myself walk away, I have a bald spot.

I'm in an alleyway blowing soap bubbles, trying to get them to float to the 10th floor of the adjacent building in the belief that, if seen, they would heal a sick friend who lies in bed by the window, but my lungs are not big enough nor strong enough and my breadth too indelicate to make the bubbles most optimum for such flight.

The family sits down to dinner. There is a condor with feet the span of dinner plates, razor savage talons, chained to the center of the table, and I am afraid to approach, whereas everyone else has hungrily begun eating.

There is a goose or a duck whose posterior feathers flump to mimic a human face.

Riding on the upper deck of the bus, the view so cycloramic makes me think of Serangoon Garden Road, but it's really Fillmore Street. In the small corner lots on city blocks, the municipality has installed new prefabbed playgrounds, all bakelite and vinyl in primary colors. Receded into the existing foliage as if they were real, polyurethane trees, six, eighteen feet high. Looking up across the way, there is a lesser panda napping in the branches of one.

Over the vista, the land is liquefying, buildings collapse methodically. But I am not surprised, nor afraid.

Book Two

THE UNHOLY GHOST

The Gutted

We were the fuck-ups or so we thought we were, lacking a system to make it through the day, much less a year, a lifetime. We clung to lifelines, like aging spiders cling to the last sticky silken thread hanging off their ass, the last chance for nourishment, protection, defense, identity. We clung to straws. With our fistfuls of clutched straw, we wove a manger, a cozy forge to call our cave a home, our shanty beachfront real estate.

We grew up to be children, infants, stillborn even. And like children of every generation, we felt it in our bones to taunt death, stick our tongues out, make monkey faces, tempt it to cross this line we drew in spit on the ground; some days we even mixed our spit to draw our never intersecting always maddening lines, we drew ever-widening concentric circles; we traintracked into our nevermores.

And like children of every generation, we tested the firmaments of our maturing bodies by vowing never to toe the line, we tested the waters of our growing up by crossing the line. The heads of our decapitated taste buds long accustomed to discount wine and day-old meat, a thousand and one tales of better feasts, desired the ravishing spill of a fresh kiss, the spurt of fresh kill, a story of our own to rival. How then could we help our bleeding gums, our gnashed chewed tongues? Oh, kiss kiss kill kill! Our blood-mixed spit-scored axis drawn, all pistons fueled, we would walk the line: we went to war, we romanced in all those chemical awe, we sought visions but settle for hallucinations lubricated in nefarious spirits, in rigorous ecstasy.

We were the atom that stubbornly refused to split, the element that secretly and selfishly held more elementary particulars. We were the Lost Boys if they had dicks to use, and understood their perverse urges, their untinkered bells. We were the Lost Boys who played Lord of the Flies and bludgeoned the annoying flighty green pipsqueak to death, set Wendy free, and declared ourselves *found*. We could not even conceive to decline, our mouths would conform to all those blowjobs but to *No*, oh no! no not never mind.

We ripped the rubbers out of their foils and made balloon animals from them, great beasts with slippery spermicidal hides. Slicked-backed pelted for every poke. We punctured, penetrated and connected end to end to the very end. A procession of rutting animals from here to the icy outer rings of Saturn. The God of Melancholy abdicated his crown. The jester wept.

We chased bugs. Such entomologists we were, even as we lacked a system of nomenclature. We would write our own field guide, we believed, and so went scouring wild in the fields and swamps with our butterfly nets and specimen jars. We substituted taxonomy with taxidermy. Our display cases were legendary. *Bug meet pin. Hello, Pin! Is that your friend Needle? Does he want to play? Ouch! You're a pokey pair, aren't you? Watch where you put your point now.*

Envious of our subjects, we joined them encase, wings spread, legs positioned, exoskeleton desiccated; pupal and larval in all we sought, we glinted chitinous and crystalline, strung up for pleasure, strung out for beauty, all our useless beauty, what were we to do with so much of it all. We were the genus and the species of an unknowable monad, a brilliant lacunae of evolution, an aporia of intelligent design. We wiped the floor and polished brass fixtures with Patagonian finches.

How the elders in their yachts on the marina, cocktails in hand, laughed and mocked as we stood at the shoreline. *Look at them, so useless in the shallow!* they tittered. Little did they consider nor care that we were preparing to wade in all the way to the deep end. En route we learned to ride barracuda, learned the finer whipping stabs of personal poison from stingray and catfish, we traded dental tips with sharks of all stripes, traded potions and recipes with fugu.

But still those ancient sun-leathered mossbacks remained unmoved, senile and contemptuous in their scorn. Did they think it all sashimi? They thought their moors solid. They did not believe in the coming storms. We wrote the weather forecasts. But still we did not have the system to move the doldrums, set gale to twister, seed the sky to rain down lava and ash.

At the impasse, we howled and bore down. We ate bullet-ridden crow. How would we reinvent the wheel, rediscover fire, redraw the orbits of the planets, recalculate the minutes in a month, the hours in a day, the years of wildness and wilderness? Pecked for vindication, we would see the boulders erode to gravel, the gravel to beach sand; construct a development of sandcastles. The very first atomic blast would turn those sandcastles into houses of crystal and glass, sparkling enough for any King to live in.

We sought shelter and peace. Our musk was survival, and our slick-back stamina. The closet optimist and the attic pessimist patiently teaching each other to paso doble in front of the hangman.

We stamped our feet and stood our ground. With our glower intact and in overdrive, we faced down God and Man and all the arms of authority, or what we thought and saw to be the armaments of authority. We did not have the system to know there was no greater God nor good, no higher authority nor flexing arm than our infinitesimal germinating selves. And when we did find out, when we found out, were found out, did we then become adults, grown-ups, the men, the women, the other, the beast, the greatest of our generation? Would the rainbow now appear and the light of the new day tan our pale skinless patties?

We ran our bodies into the ground trusting we would heal, we would resurrect, trusting we would regain strength, composure, might. We are the gutted and the chawed. Our conga line was glorious on Monday, invincible by Wednesday, cortege by Friday and when weekend rolls around, after fasting on Friday, feasting and fucking on Saturday and all-day Church on Sunday, we regroup and we become glorious if not quite whole again in the new week.

We found each other time and again, over and over, even when there was no one else left in the world and all the earth was a wasteland. That was what we did. That was all we did, we, the sweating and the saved.

And all it took was for one of us to fall. And our babbling mouths so full of tongues oh so foul and mighty could not handle it: "...left this life, caught his last, left the stage, left us suddenly, passed away, communes with the spirits, passed away peacefully, made his journey home, suffers no longer, succumbed, passed peacefully from this life into God's hands, soul left, last eternal voyage, departed, left us..."

We choked. We phlegmed. We asphyxiated. We sprouted dragging third left feet and stumbled over them. We dominoes had no recourse but to clack and fall. And oh, we held on tight to each other, hoping for ballast in our fusion, for root to take earth, and arms length to trade. How do the drowning clutch at floating bendy straws? The same way they would at the uprooted Angsana floating by, at every little nookery of each life's debris floating down the meander. The ox-bow will be decades in the forming.

We held on so tight to one another in the days of our floods, and our embrace was sufficient buttress, if only there was bedrock.

All it takes is a death so close, it is like bringing all you hold dear to the edge of the mightiest cliff and tossing the first piece over, then watching each succeeding piece be the lemming of the next, a one and a one going over, knowing you'll never ever see those pieces again, never reassemble in glory or shame; if you had any salt left, you would weep for every single piece that plunges into the breaking surf, you are no cliff diver nor pearl hunter. All it takes is going to the water's edge and surrendering the elegantly carved pieces of yourself to the physics of surface tension, only to stand back and watch thumb-sucking as you drown. Knowing that you are, no, not powerless, but incomprehensible to do a damn thing. Not a goddamned thing, but God doesn't want any part of this, does he?

All it takes is one so close it might even be yourself.

The path is littered with banana peels and anthills, diamonds and oxide, scripture and stress tests, crack and crybabies, teachers and tar babies, bullets and uncounted ballots, wedding rings and cedar coffins, deeds and donefors.

The beach is glorious, in plain view. And there we stand.

Our bonfires guttering.

We, the gutted.

I, the gutted.

Chicken Little

With the sky fallen,
with my tail feathers drooped and flumped
I stand at the edge of the great pit,
matched only by the one in my stomach
grinding by my gizzards.
In the cineplex, I'm a hero,
saving the world from annihilation,
but here, I'm just some diseased cluck.
Why us? Why do the canaries,
the sparrows and pigeons, the parakeets
get a free ride? If only you knew
what those pretty songbirds hide
in their diseased throats, under their pretty
feathers. And it's more than a sniffle,
or a flu, I can tell you that.

At daybreak, they will round up all my kind,
herd them into this great hole, pour bags of lime over them
disregarding the panic, and push dirt in, bury them
alive. When the boots and tractors and gawkers are gone,
who will hear the turned soil's muted cluckering.
Tell me again the sky hasn't fallen.
But that is the lot of my peeps.
We face fire. We always have.
Unfortunately, when we pass through fire,
we become fantastically tasty.

Shocked, Awed

Do not punish the innocent
for the innocent.

      ★★★

To those who fight them, all wars are holy wars.
The processes and machinations not so holy.
The straggling few who begin unholy
start inside the warrior's hearts.

      ★★★

"I wouldn't like to live in America but sometimes I would."
— Georges Perec, *On the Difficulty of Imagining an Ideal City*

      ★★★

Put your guns down.
Lay bare your arms.
Sleep your head down.
Wake to dream unharmed.

      ★★★

The Photos:
What is it, Jung said, about the healthy man
does not torture others, it is
the tortured who turn into torturers.
Predictable the defense,
could have almost seen it captioned
under the photo: Following Orders.

As if any order can void being human.
But no defense or denial can argue
against those smirks smugly branding
the faces of the perpetrators.

We know the difference between good and evil.
Between inflicting pain and not.
Between bargaining with the devil
and bargaining with the devil.

Somewhere, in this country, those scenes
are being reenacted in someone's bedroom.
Somewhere, someone is masturbating to them.
He may feel guilt and shame
or he may be bargaining.

This is our deal: How
do we know what hasn't been photographed,
what we haven't yet cannot see?
Does the imagination seize in suspicion
and grade harsh, mild,
justified,
or not at all?

                        ***

"It may sometimes be hard to define good, but evil has its unmistakable odor."
                        — Amos Oz, *Goethe Prize Lecture, 2005*

                        ***

Here: 9/11
Everywhere else: 11/9

                        ***

The Memorial:
Sharpie on cardboard
a Beanie Baby
two plastic daisies
his dogtags.

On the roadside

at the crossroads
marked by blood and tears.

Trampled by feet fleeing
Soon to be swept by the hot night
winds into the desert.

See the blood burrowing to its ferrous home.
See the tears nesting in one seed's testa,
waiting for the rainy season.

★★★

Vessel:
The pathology of blood, when innocent, is pure and potent.
If unjustly shed, it flows unclottingly.
A hemorrhage that can overnight stain an entire mountain range.
This is the litmus.
The mountains and their associated ski resorts will be re-christened in
    commemoration.
Fungus will be scaled off all the bronze memorials, new flags will be
    flown.
The pathology of blood in guilt is never witnessed by human eyes.

★★★

"No man is an island, entire of itself; every man is a piece of the
continent, a part of the main… Any man's death diminishes me, because
I am involved in mankind…" John Donne, *Meditation XVII*

★★★

Everything is known to us.

Boxing Day, 2004

When the tide goes out as it does
faithful as clockwork,
the beach is awash with mud-bloated bodies
dotting the endless shore of debris,
each belly distended and all
eerily the same clay-stained color;
some naked, others clinging on
to the bits and drabs of clothing
not stripped off by currents, but all,
their extremities partially eaten
by crabs and iguanas, tide-hungry fish,
now being pecked at by gulls and terns
and pigeons and even the sparrows
want their bit of pluck.
Someone will come swinging
an umbrella or a broom, shooing
those hungry birds away, and more
will join swinging and swatting away –
might as well put on boxing gloves
to punch at a wave, or take a cricket bat to crest;
but never mind – until arms
tire in the swelter and day's
calling pulls inland.
The bodies will be retrieved
before the tide returns, and it does,
punctual and picking the littered sprawl
riding flotsam on its calm splashing spine,
depositing more bodies and more wreckage on ebb.
The beach will eventually be cleared,
the sands baked shell white as ever
if not ever unsoiled.
And we will tell the children
that there's nothing to be afraid of.
That it's okay to eat fish.
That it's okay to picnic, to play
in the surf and tidepools, to make sandcastles

and dig for clams. We want them to enjoy
the beach like we did when we were
that age when there was nothing to
be afraid of.

The Week in SARS

It's not so easy to breathe in the N95 Particle Respirator Mask, the box
of which took more than five weeks to get; backordered till Labor Day,
the sales rep wearily informs all callers. From the first breath, the
condensation collects within, and on your snout: such clammy
conditions just right for fungal infections to take root. Mr. Ringworm
licks its whatever-passes-for-lips-in-fungi. Then your glasses fog up, and
all day fight your nose bridge for territory to hang to. But in public for
the first weeks, we wouldn't take it off. We held our breaths more than
we should have. We scowled at the coughing as we suppressed even the
urge to clear a throat. We learned to breathe again.

      ★★★

Do you want to die? And I don't mean a nice lay-in-bed-covered-with-
fresh-flower-petals-with-family-&-friends-bedside-to-see-you-off die.
This is a hazmat-team-whisks-you-off-to-a-restricted-area-of-the-
hospital-where-your-family-cannot-visit-not-that-they-can-since-
they're-in-quarantine-for-the-month-as-well-instantly-cremated-&-*here-
you-go,-here's-the-ashes* die.

      ★★★

Little strips of plastic stuck to the middle of the forehead
on all the congregated in the auditorium.
            Sci-Fi Bindi? Futuristic Third-Eye?

Just plain cheaply mass-produced in China throw-away thermometers.

The bit of plastic black slowly turns green,
as if photosynthesis were taking place,
nothing so complicated though,
just a normal human body
simmering in its own warm life.

A throng of dark eyes
flinting around the room,
nervously waiting

for those who
        turn red.

    ***

First day of school ever, first school uniform.
Above the school crest patch, a sticker:
Blue smiley-face gumming a popsicle-thermometer,
proclaiming, I'm Cool!
And over Mr. Cool's face: 36; written
in Sharpie: the child's body temperature, recorded
before she's dropped off, during third period,
before recess, and seventh period.

    ***

"I did not know Louis Vuitton made surgical masks. Or Burberry's."

"They don't."

    ***

The moment the Fasten Seatbelts Sign was turned off, everyone shuffled
up and about to claim a whole row of seats for themselves. This will
prove tricky when we have to tell the officer at the immigration
checkpoint our exact seat number *retained for four weeks for future tracking
purposes.*

    ***

The airport luminal
in its almost clinical
steel and glass patina
hangs on to
an almost movie-like eerie
quietness.

You're nearly gone.
Or almost home.

Unbecoming

I belong to that generation of my country
that was Americanized way before we were
Americanized. And when I say
we were Americanized, I mean to say we were
      British-ized, German-ized, Australian-ized, French-ized;

the more ambitious managed to be Scandinavian-ized,
and hardly anyone was Canadian-ized for some reason.

All much to the dismay
of the anthropologists disguised as tourists
who came armed with their cameras and assorted prodding apparatuses.
They fumed: *Surely the young must know something more folksy,*
           what will we do for our thesis, dissertation, tenure,
           book/film project, slide-show, post-academic career
           as cruise ship resident docent to strange
           yet fascinating, different yet unthreatening cultures?

The businessmen however were joyful.
The military fraternized.
          The workers worked,
the hookers hooked,
          the tourists toured,
the shoppers bargained,
          and everyone cried out for more.

What we knew of the United States,
          of The West,
came from TV, the movies, and the supermarket.
Fuzzy notions and grand ideas:
          Freedom (available
in red, white, blue, diet, decaffeinated, classic, cherry & lo-carb).
Of speech, assembly; opposition without reprisals,
no one was detained or imprisoned without trial,
          imagine that.

This was a place of high crime & lofty courts & wacky lawsuits.
This was a place where the individual ruled.
Wild wooly homosexuals roamed the streets in packs.
Everything was up for sale or auction with a payment plan.
There was a chocolate bar, a crate of Pepsi, a handgun,
& the newest Schwarzenegger DVD on every dinner table.
Dinner was being delivered by some other immigrant.

                    ★★★

If you go west and keep going,
you get to the east, then back from where you started.
                    (Unless you've been torpedoed by anti-aircraft missiles
                                in the interest of national security.)
Two of my uncles are sitting in the living room,
they yearn for the year 2020 when they believe
China "will be great again";
            oh! how they long to get a glimpse of that.
One is planning to immigrate to the motherland
to teach English. The other doesn't travel well
because of shrapnel sustained during the Japanese Occupation.
My jibe that the Three Gouges Dam and the 2008 Olympics will crush
China's infrastructure does not sit well.

    ...too Americanized already, the Uncles tut.

            ★★★

What is it to be American?

It is to be resigned
to the daily over-saturation

            fat, food, diets, beauty tips, news, information, celebrity,
            pleasure, discounts, self-help, advertising, product,
            choice, god, panaceas, sentimentality, nostalgia.

All of which presumably fuses
to create a shortened memory span.
Oh, for the days when terror was the summer
of the Shark Attack.
                    And *that* contested election
seemed a lifetime ago, and even now,
seems like a lifetime past.
Maybe numbness and dread creates
such time-warping effects.

It is to cling to singularities, to shun simultaneity.
A singular pursuit of happiness, a singular map
and measure of the world, a singular culture
dictating a singular morality.

It is to be resigned
to a culture that encourages the simplification
of reality, even as its products keep supersizing,
and its needs and desires expand.

It is to be contented
to live in childlike states of ignorance.
To worship brawn over brain, to prefer
wholesome ignorance over knowledge.
Feelings fuel the kiln that forge the Golden Calf.

It is to stubbornly refuse
to rise to the bar, demanding that the bar
be reforged in flexible plastic and then being
insulted to be in the presence of a bar
that doesn't serve a recognizable American beer.

It is to refuse to see
the whole picture, to turn away
from the unpleasant, the discomforting, the genitals,
then using what is seen, transcripted
as the gold of experience,
to form whole flaws into myths into truths.

It is to be unable to grasp context, irony, ambiguities,
while fully capable of feeding the unicorn at the petting zoo;
it is to be able to justify all illogicalities with God,
government, greed and guns. The delusion of power,
of individuality, of One Nation Under God.

It is a seat at the table
with a pasteurized version of the world served up on the placemat.

Oh, the absurdity of it all
                                        would be so funny
if the villagers weren't sharpening their pitchforks,
preparing the pyre and the noose, and already going
door to door with their lighted torches,
while subcommittees are en route to neighboring towns.

                          ★★★

In August of 2003, after years
of filling and filing inscrutable form after form,
I was finally called in for my Citizenship interview.

Two days before the interview,
I realized that I still did not quite know
a few of the middle lines to the National Anthem.
At sporting events, you can possibly par-sing along
with the masses, but solo, it's a syntactic nightmare.
Like the true American I was to be,
I rushed to my computer and downloaded a version that I could
listen to repeatedly, learn from.
In retrospect, I should have picked someone
other than Cyndi Lauper who herself was cribbing from Marvin Gaye.

I imagined the interview would be like *Wheel of Fortune*,
            "I'd like to buy an E!"
but as it turns out, it's more like
The Price is Right, or possibly, *Jeopardy*.

The night before, my mom calls and sternly warns me,
             "Just give them the right answers;
          this is not the time to try make a point."

Yes, there are right answers.

Section IX, question 5:
Name one positive result of the Watergate affair during Nixon's Presidency.

My head was swimming with answers.[1]

For some reason, I expected
the test to be much more difficult
than the twenty short questions that it was.
For the better part of the year in preparation,
I had been cramming up on U.S. history, politics and government.
The guidebook the then-INS provided to applicants was written
during the Bush administration — the first Bush administration:
the list of presidents and their accomplishments stopped at Reagan.
The word "surreal" is vastly overused in the vernacular.
But this was surreal.

To read about the principled blueprint
of separating church and state, the scrutiny
over governmental powers, the system of checks & balances,
the Bill of Rights, the hard-worn architecture
of this tattered democracy
we hold in our laps,
             all this while outside, on the far side
of the continent, at the other shining sea,
one war bleeds into another, blended
into an indistinguishable bloody mess.

---

1. The correct one, according to the model answers provided, apparently, is: *The encouraging result of Watergate was a confirmation that the American democratic form of government worked even under such negative conditions. It showed that the Constitution and the American system of government was strong enough for even the President to be held accountable for his actions.*

Shock & Awe becomes a spangly videogame
or an anti-acne regiment.
>   *And lo! what is to come:*
A generation of this country on prosthetics,
shell-shocked.

Here is the church, here is the steeple,
open the door and out flood its people, determined
to nest in every dining, bed and boardroom,
as they have been commanded to.
But of course, the objection is never
so much their Christian doctrine
as much as their absence of Christian virtue.

Here, more people are being arrested on scant evidence and sent
to lockdowns, secret prisons in diplomatically contentious countries
awaiting trails that never come. *Kafkaesque,*
it's often termed, often by the very same folk
who would also call it "surreal."
For the idea itself
seemed to come from the realm of fiction set in a foreign country.

Here, we-the-people
have no concept of freedom's absence,
cannot imagine
the cogs of daily lives without it.
>   So accustomed
to its breeze on every face.
It is unquestioned. Like limbs and any appendage,
its presence is given,
>   even if they have to be phantom limbs.
It is presumed that if surrendered, given away,
it can always be reclaimed, recovered,
it will be given back.

It seems that so many citizens
are more than willing to give up their rights –
rights their country was trying to cram down other's throats –
all for a roll of sparkly American flag stickers.

There is a disquieting tumor latent
in the nucleus of every American Dream,
threatening to unleash its specter.

Fear and paranoia beget vulgar nationalism.

Now, the military budget swells to monster
movie proportions; secret tribunals, interrogations
and torture conducted by the military and their hired private guns
all in our name and in service of our cherished security,
barely raise a heckle.

I want to call this evil,
but evil is what you talk about
when you cannot explain what is happening.

And if truth be told,
the times we live in have always been
the times lived in.
    That old cliché about
not learning from history and thus repeating it.
If only there was agreement in the lesson plan,
standardized testing.
    Wash, rinse, repeat.
The history of the world, in all
its orbit seasons of social order and disorder,
is an ever slow gathering of dark forces
that emanates from our blooded meridians,

and it is our light, our essential dignity,
that we believe better and otherwise.

Cue the reruns; The remakes are playing
louder and on a higher rota.

       "In Modern America, no nightmare is forbidden."
          — JG Ballard, *The Guardian May 14, 2004*

In America, every insanity demands
a witness, its own audience.

In the middle of the road,
all we really have is a consumer's democracy.

We create monsters and then live in such dizzying fear of them.

We create Gods who abandon us in our time of need.

We worship Gods who demand more than our capacity of grace.

And at the end of the road,
America doesn't exist,
it is just a name that you give to an abstract idea.

But that's the difference between history booked and history lived.

I stand corrected.
This was not surreal.
This was sad.

This was frustrating and despairing.
This was frightening.

I am more afraid of my government
than I am of terrorists
and what acts they might commit in my city.

★★★

A Green Card is not actually green;
at J Crew, it is Dune mixed with Quartz;
at the more conservative Banana Republic, it is Apricot
with hints of British Khaki.
If you look at the back of a Green Card, you will see
little dots above the golden swipe strip.
Look closely,

each of these dots is actually a miniature silhouette portrait
of every American president to the current one
when the card was issued.

I have lived in this country for a third of my life.
And in this time, coming and going on numerous occasions,
I've had to cross that border, that invisible imaginary
and all-powerful line that separates
here and there,
                    us and them.

This has happened to me only once ever,
but it has stayed with me all this time.

One clear morning, coming back
into the country at San Francisco International Airport,
the immigration official looked at my passport,
he checked my photo.
He swiped in the data and checked it,
he stamped my passport and signed the stamp,
he returned my documents to me,
and then,
            he said, *Welcome home.*

And I knew I loved this place once again.

Acknowledgments

The author wishes to thank Lisa Asagi, R. Zamora Linmark, Lori Takeyesu, Morgan Blair, Tod La Ron, Dave Thomson, Lattlé Pussby, Manic D Press, and my lovely family. I am also grateful to the Kimmel Harding Nelson Center for the Arts in Nebraska City.

About the Author

Justin Chin was born in Malaysia and raised in Singapore. He is the author of two poetry collections, *Bite Hard* and *Harmless Medicine*, as well as two collections of personal essays, *Burden of Ashes* and *Mongrel*, and a collection of performance texts, *Attack of the Man-Eating Lotus Blossoms*. The poetry collection *Harmless Medicine* was a finalist in the Bay Area Book Reviewers Association Awards, and the Publishing Triangle Awards. Chin currently lives in San Francisco.

About the Text

The title poem, *Gutted*, is loosely structured after the Japanese poetic form, *zuihitsu*. Formless in its form, the *zuihitsu* takes on any numbers of styles and forms — diary entries, lists, quotations, observations, commentaries, fragments — and is as much a way of thinking as it is poetic form. Literally translated, *zuihitsu* describes a text that "follows the brush." In contemporary times, it has been described as Japanese pillow book, occasional writings, random thoughts, or miscellany.